FIRST EDITIONS AND FINAL WORDS

An estate sale windfall, a forged colophon, a confession in the margins.

Copyright © 2025 by Ivy Grant

Cover designed by Azameti Michael

Published by Azameti Michael

All rights reserved. No part of this book may be reproduced, distributed, or transmitted in any form or by any means, electronic or mechanical, including photocopying, recording, or any information storage and retrieval system, without the prior written permission of the publisher, except in the case of brief quotations embodied in critical reviews and certain other non-commercial uses permitted by copyright law.

This is a work of fiction. Names, characters, places, and incidents are either the product of the author's imagination or used fictitiously. Any resemblance to actual persons, living or dead, or actual events is purely coincidental.

For information about this title or to request permission for use, please contact:

greyama70@gmail.com

First Edition, 2025

BOOK THREE

PEPPERMINT CAT BOOKSHOP MYSTERIES

TABLE OF CONTENTS

Chapter 1: Estate Rush
Chapter 2: Pricing Dance
Chapter 3: Colophon Doubt
Chapter 4: Deckle Shave
Chapter 5: Seller Missing
Chapter 6: Printer Past
Chapter 7: Margin Dates
Chapter 8: Phone Spine
Chapter 9: Book Club Brag
Chapter 10: Ink Age
Chapter 11: Blade Nick
Chapter 12: Press Visit
Chapter 13: Car Trunk
Chapter 14: Meet in the Stacks
Chapter 15: Footage Frame
Chapter 16: Printer Admits
Chapter 17: Host Cracks
Chapter 18: Recovery
Chapter 19: Restitution
Chapter 20: Final Words
ABOUT THE AUTHOR

CHAPTER 1

Estate Rush

The bell on the door rang like a small permission. Morning sun slid across the front table and put a bright edge on the display sign. Peppermint took that as a cue and leapt from the poetry shelf to the counter, tail high, whiskers forward. He did not land. He sailed. He surveyed his kingdom, gave me one blink, and planted himself next to the receipt spike like a supervisor with paws.

Talia Brooks wrestled a cardboard box through the doorway and bumped it closed with her hip. The box was taped twice and labeled in block letters. Firsts. She was twenty at most, hair in a knot that had lost the fight. Worry had hands on her shoulders.

"Do I need an appointment," she said, breath short.

"You brought one," I said. "It is the heavy thing with tape."

She tried to smile and did not pull it off. She dragged the box across the rug and set it on the counter. The carton sagged at one corner where old tape had given up. Peppermint put one paw on it like a notary seal.

"I am Talia," she said. "My aunt is cleaning her house. I am supposed to help. I do not know how to do this part."

"You came to the right place," I said. "I am Liora. You can put the rest on the floor. We start with one."

"There are two more in the car," she said. "And a milk crate that stabbed me. I hate milk crates."

"Rafi," I called.

He came from the back with a towel over his shoulder and a tray of cups in his hands. He took one look at the box and at Talia's face and set the tray down without clink. He held the door and fetched the other boxes with a gait that said he had done this before and would do this again. He returned with the crate and a raised eyebrow for the way the plastic had tried to eat his knuckles.

Peppermint circled the first box and sat on the lid. He does that when the day wants a gavel. I slid a box cutter under the tape and lifted the flaps. Paper dust breathed up. The smell was good. Cloth and glue and years.

On top sat a title that makes grown collectors start talking in footnotes. Jacket intact. Board corners true. The paper edges looked raw and beautiful at first glance, deckle swollen in the way people like to name in listings. I moved it under the task lamp and set two fingers to the fore edge.

Too smooth. Not that gentle ragged comb old stock gives you. This edge had been shaved. Someone had run a light hand along a blade to clean it up. I did not flinch. It is rude to grimace at a gift.

"Where did these come from," I asked.

"My aunt's study," Talia said. "A neighbor passed and left her shelves. She is downsizing. I am trying to get tuition in order for fall. I picked books that looked important and wrote Firsts because I saw it in a list online and it seemed like a word that made sense."

"Who else has seen this box," I asked.

"An estate guy," she said. "He came with the people who price furniture. He said he could help us not get taken. He was fast."

I flipped the top book to the back and checked the colophon.

Clean mark. Too clean. Ink density wrong for a true impression. The dot grid sat a half step off center. Not obvious. Enough for a loupe to sing about it. I did not take out the loupe yet.

"Name," I asked.

"Seth Marlowe," she said. "He knows auctions. He wears a jacket that smells like cedar."

That tracked. Seth likes rooms where he can talk first and invoice later. He calls it help. He calls a lot of things help.

"When did he look," I said.

"Yesterday," she said. "He said he could take the boxes to someone. I said no. He frowned. He took a picture of the fancy one and told me not to let anyone touch it until we agreed to a price." She paused, then added, "He also told me the market turns fast and fear makes you poor."

"Fear also keeps you from signing bad slips," I said.

Peppermint swatted the edge of the jacket with one paw and pulled back as if the paper had hissed. He leaned and sniffed the fore edge. He sneezed once, sharp. He did not care for something.

I peeled a piece of tissue from the box and lifted the next book. Good binding. Wrong spine stamp for the supposed run. I turned it. The label pressed a little too shallow. I noted it without announcing it. I set it aside.

"Let me show you how we start," I said. "We log what you brought. We fix a chain. We do not let anyone whisk anything anywhere. We do not chase a number. We compare to sales that closed, not to dreams."

Talia nodded the way people nod when they have never seen a rope bridge but have decided to cross one.

I wrote the date in the intake book and put her name in the left column, the one that holds responsibility like a hand. I logged the box count and the crate and the first title, then the other spines I could see without digging. I placed the top book on a foam cradle and put on gloves. Not for show. For oil. I set a weight on the hinge and opened to the colophon again.

Miss Dotty Bell chose that moment to glide in from the sidewalk. She wears a felt hat no matter the month and dates type by sight like a parlor trick that has been sharpened on a thousand labels. She pretended to browse, which is what she does when she plans to watch me work.

"Morning," she said to Peppermint first, which is correct, then to me. "I saw the boxes. I did not trip anyone with my cane. I deserve a parade."

She leaned on the counter and peered. I slid the book so the colophon sat under the task light.

"What do you think," I asked in the voice you use when you want truth and not theater.

Her mouth went flat. "I think that press never threw a mark that thin," she said. "Look at the low dots. See how they drift. Real letterpress would give them a different kind of flaw. This reads like offset trying to pass. And the ink is too even. This decade's ink smiles for cameras. That decade did not."

Talia gripped the edge of the counter with both hands. "Is it fake," she said.

"It is something," I said. "We will find out what. That is why I am writing things down."

The bell spoke again and in slid Seth Marlowe, jacket worn open to catch air, cologne a notch too high, smile in place. He tipped two fingers at Talia like a head waiter and put his phone on the counter like a challenge coin.

"I was in the area," he said. "Figured I would check on my favorite student."

"Your favorite student said no to moving these boxes yesterday," I said. "They are logged here now. They are staying here until we sort them."

"That depends on whether you know what you are looking at," he said. He kept the smile. He has practiced in a mirror.

"I do," I said.

He glanced at the book on the cradle and at the colophon. He did not lean too close. He knows the rule in this room. Hands off unless told otherwise.

"First state," he said. "That is a windfall for a girl about to start classes. If it is real."

"If," I said.

He unlocked his phone with his thumb and brought up a photo. My book. My title. Yesterday's date stamped at the top. The spine stamp on his shot did not match the one on our board. The placement differed. His photo showed a deeper bite. Either he shot a different copy or something changed between then and now.

He angled the screen so Talia could see. "I told you to bring the lot to me," he said. "I have buyers who act. Shops linger. By the time you get done with your ink tests and your little magnifying glass, the number will be gone. Tuition will keep being tuition."

"You have buyers who like panic," I said. "I have shelves that like to stand up straight."

He put the phone down and drummed one finger next to it. "I can take that box next door right now. I will have an offer on your email in an hour. Cash tomorrow. No time for cold feet."

I did not look at Talia. I kept my eyes on him. I put my hand on the intake book so the timestamp would be in frame for the corner camera.

"This is a consignment shop," I said. "We consign. We research. We sell. We do not hand boxes to men who take pictures and vanish."

He turned the smile on me. "You think I am a thief."

"I think you are a rush," I said. "I do not give keys to the person who just told me to drive faster."

He huffed and tried to make it a laugh. He slid his phone into his jacket and lifted his hands. "I am trying to help. There is a lot of trash floating around this week. Forged marks. New ink pretending to be old. You will get burned if you play with things you do not understand."

"We will see," I said.

"I will be at the diner," he said. "For an hour. Tell me you changed your mind. I can still move lunch for you."

He touched two fingers to his temple like a salute to a stage light and left. The bell said the sentence he wanted as a flourish. I did not give it to him.

Talia stared at the door for three seconds and then looked at me as if my face could do math. "I cannot lose this chance," she said. "If even part of this box is real, I can cover the gap and not have to pick up a third shift. My aunt thinks tuition grows on trees."

"It grows on paper," I said. "Slow paper."

I set the book back on the cradle and pulled the loupe. I kept my hand steady so she could see that the tool is not magic. It is a small lens and a quiet mind.

"See the dots," I said. "See how the pattern leans. See how the ink pools at the left of the tiny circles, then goes thin. This press prints its mark different. I will take a macro and send it to a foreman who used to run that room. He will tell me if I am right."

She leaned in. "I can almost see it," she said. "I cannot afford for you to be wrong."

"I cannot afford it either," I said. "This shop runs on repeat business and long memory. People bring me boxes because my slips hold up in the light."

She nodded, once, slow. "What about the edge," she asked.

I ran my finger along the fore edge again. Not rough. Not natural. Too sleek where it should show air.

"Deckle feels like a cliff trail," I said. "This feels like someone dragged a small knife and thought no one would know. Theo will put a blade in his hand and show you the pass. We will check for wobble where a hand corrected. If I find it, I log it."

Peppermint decided his part required motion. He hopped from the counter to the cradle and stood with one paw on the cloth joint, nose an inch from the paper. He took a breath and sneezed again, a sharp little bark of opinion. He stepped back and looked offended that the book had been under his nose at all.

"Do you need me to call my aunt," Talia asked. "She is out with her book club. They meet late. She said she would bring me a cookie and then she never came home and I do not want to be the reason anyone is mad."

"You are not the reason for anything," I said. "Call her. If she does not pick up, call her neighbor. If you still do not get an answer, text me the last time you heard from her. I will call Asa."

She pulled out her phone with hands that could not decide between speed and care. She dialed. The call went to voicemail. She tried again. I watched her throat move once when she swallowed.

"Leave a message," I said. "Bright voice. Ask her to call the shop. Then give me her neighbor's name."

She did. She looked less like a person on a rope bridge now and more like a person in a small boat looking for a dock.

Miss Dotty tilted her head and pointed her cane at the book. "Look at page thirteen," she said.

I turned to thirteen. Near the bottom margin, a tiny curl in the paper marked where a blade had drifted and then corrected. No one would see it without want. It was there.

"Good eye," I said.

"I have two," she said. "Both still work."

I pulled the intake camera on the counter closer so the lens would catch the page and the wobble and my pencil when I wrote the note. I put it on the line with a date and a time and a short phrase. Fore edge shave. Wobble at 13. Pending. Then I slid the book into a mylar sleeve and set a red tag on top. Hold.

I bagged a macro photo of the colophon dot grid and wrote the case number on the corner of the print.

Talia's phone buzzed. She listened, then frowned. "Voicemail again," she said. "Her car keys are usually on a hook by the door. She is the kind of person who never loses a key. I have never not heard from her after a club night."

"Text me her address," I said. "I will go after lunch if Asa is not already there. For now, your job is to breathe. Rafi will make you tea. Peppermint will judge you for putting your bag on his stool. We will get through the stack and then you can watch me write stiff emails to people who wear ties."

She slid onto the stool and put her bag on the floor. Peppermint approved. Rafi poured hot water over a bag and set the cup on a saucer that had seen a better day. He put a cookie next to it because morale is a food group. He carried the milk crate to the back without letting it bite him.

I went through the next box. A couple of strong midlist titles. A signed local that always sells fast. One cookbook with a jacket stain that looks like pepper oil and will not wash out. The kind of box that keeps the lights on when a windfall turns out to be a breeze.

At the bottom, under a sheaf of tissue that stuck to my fingers, sat a smaller book wrapped in a plastic sleeve that smelled like the back of a school closet. I slit the tape and slid it free. The paper felt right in weight and wrong in surface. I turned it under the lamp and saw a faint sheen. Someone had burnished the boards to make them read new. The spine stamp tried to pass and did not.

"Did the estate guy handle this one," I asked.

"I do not know," Talia said. "He was quick. He had me bring them to the kitchen while the furniture people measured the table and argued with a cousin about who gets the tea set. I wanted to go to bed."

"You did fine," I said. "You brought them to a counter that keeps chain. It is the least glamorous answer and the only one that pays."

The door opened and Asa Quinn stepped in without the bell needing to work hard. He nodded at me, at Peppermint, at the intake book. He read my face at a glance and did not ask in front of the room.

"Morning," he said to Talia. "I am Asa with the sheriff. Are you Talia. I got your text from Ms. Wren. You tried your aunt twice and then called her neighbor."

"Yes," she said. "I do not want to be dramatic. She does this club thing and comes home late and eats toast and tells me who made a speech. Today she did not come home."

"Give me the address," he said. "Sit tight. Do not hand any boxes to anyone in a hurry. Ms. Wren will keep a lid on the book side."

He left with a nod I have seen before. Quiet. Sure. He does not run the siren if the road is dry and the tires touch.

Peppermint pressed his head against Talia's wrist and purred once, a short engine that says unit cohesion. She let out a breath. She looked at the book in the cradle and at the box on the floor and at the door Asa had just used. Her mouth was steady now.

"What if none of these are real," she said.

"Then we sell what is solid and we write a better plan for fall," I said. "You do not strap yourself to one book. You strap yourself to work. If one is real, we get a better number because we did not rush. If two are fake, we keep someone else from paying a price for a lie. That is worth something you can spend later."

She nodded again. The nod was better this time. Less fear. More spine.

I closed the cradle and slid the top book back into its sleeve. I wrote one more line in the intake book. Photo received of different spine stamp, prior day. Source: Seth. Logged 10:27. I signed the line with the small flourish I reserve for notes that may end up on a projector in a room where the chairs do not match.

Miss Dotty tapped her cane as if calling the class to order. "You will test the ink," she said.

"I will," I said. "I will look at the pen stroke on the margin and at the way the dye sits. If it is a gel from eight years ago, the stroke will tell me so."

"Then I will be back at two," she said. "I will bring lunch. It is easier to see dots if you have soup."

Peppermint approved. He likes any plan that involves soup because soup includes laps.

Rafi returned from the back with a roll of fresh mylar and the long ruler we use to cut sleeves. He set them down next to the cradle and took the milk crate apart with a touch that kept his skin whole. He can charm metal.

"Do we consign," Talia asked. "Do we sign something. I do not want to take your time if you think this is a sink."

"We consign," I said. "We sign. We make a list that matches reality. You leave with a copy and a timeline. We do not promise a number we cannot name yet. We do promise that no one will walk out the door with your box while you blink."

She wiped the corner of her eye with a sleeve and nodded, once, as if pinning down a page in wind. She reached for the pen by the intake book and stopped herself like a person in a museum who almost touched a vase. I slid the form toward her and turned the pen so she could see the click. She signed where it said name and where it said address and where it said share and where it said do you want publicity. She checked no. Good.

The bell rang again and this time it was a courier with a padded sleeve for a customer and a grin. He saw the boxes and the cradle and warmed his hands on the air.

"Busy morning," he said.

"Reading day," I said.

He left and the room inhaled and then exhaled. The light shifted across the front table. The banned display held steady.

Peppermint jumped to the stool under the plant and curled into a ring that looked like a comma. I like commas. They keep sentences honest.

I took a macro of the colophon and a second of the deckle wobble and set both on the evidence mat with the case number and today's paper. I bagged them and wrote the time. I wrote the shop phone number on a sticky for Talia to send to her aunt's neighbor. I texted Theo to come in early with his knife. I pinged the old press foreman for a sample sheet scan from the right year. I ignored a message from Seth that said time is a thief and chose not to reply with a line about thieves who wear cedar.

Then I slid the top book into a hold box with clean foam and a red tag that says pause. I stacked three other titles for sunlight, the kind that can handle a quick pass on the counter with a price that will pay for tea and tape and patience. Work likes progress even when the big glass door in front of it sticks.

Talia sipped her tea and looked at the door again as if she could make Asa walk through it by will alone. Peppermint opened one eye and shut it. Rafi turned the kettle back on because we were going to need it. I wrote one more note in my hand the way I like to write when the day will get looked at later.

Intake frozen pending checks. Do not release to anyone. Logged on camera.

I set the pen down and felt the room lean toward order. In this shop, that is the sound of a day doing its best. Outside, a delivery truck groaned. Inside, the front table waited for me to set three paperbacks faced out. I did. Spine. Face. Spine. Peppermint approved this also. He has standards.

The bell did not ring. The phone did not trill. The boxes sat and looked harmless. They were not. They were a map, and I had put my finger on the first cross street. The rest would come.

The door swung open. Asa stepped back in. He had that face he uses when he has news that is not clean. He nodded at me once. He kept his voice low and steady.

"House is empty," he said. "Keys still on a hook. Car missing. I am calling it in. Keep that book caged. I will be back."

"Copy," I said.

He left. The bell spoke.

"Okay," I said to Talia. "Now we really log the chain."

She nodded. Peppermint jumped to the counter and tapped the red tag with his paw like a seal. We got back to work.

CHAPTER 2

Pricing Dance

We moved the box to the rare nook, away from the espresso thrum and the easy impulse tables. The nook holds light like a slow breath. Cloth mats line the counter. The glass case hums at a low pitch that says the temperature will not warp a hinge today. I clicked on the task lamp, a steady circle that flatters no lie.

Talia hovered with her arms crossed tight, then caught herself and tucked her hands into the back pockets of her jeans as if to keep them from touching anything they should not. Peppermint padded in, chose the broad sill by the small leaded window, and folded himself into a cinnamon comma to watch.

"First rule," I said. "Price against closed sales, not wish lists. One book at a time. No hero moves, no panic moves."

She swallowed and nodded. "I need a number that pays for statistics," she said. "And rent on a room that smells less like the inside of a refrigerator."

"We will aim for both," I said. "We will also aim for sleep."

I set the suspect title on the cradle again, eased the weight onto the gutter, and let the board lie flat. No press. No breath held long. I laid a clean card on the counter and wrote three columns across the top. Points, proof, comps. The pencil suits this kind of morning. Ink likes to commit. Pencil likes to learn.

"Points first," I said. "Edition statements, jacket price, spine stamp, colophon shape, paper edge, any oddities that belong and any oddities that do not. We will collect the truth before we look at numbers."

Talia leaned in. "Do you want me to read to you," she asked, trying for light.

"Please do," I said.

She read the edition line and the imprint and the numbers that want you to believe they are a first state. Her voice steadied as she moved across the type. Reading relieves people who grew up in houses where noise rarely helped.

"I have seen this title on lists with an eye-watering figure," she said, softer. "I should not say that where the cash drawer can hear me, but I did."

I smiled. "I talk to the cash drawer more than you think," I said. "It does not scare easy."

We checked the jacket price and the code on the flap. The ink told one story, the paper told another. I wrote the flap code on the card and put a dot by it for later. The spine stamp again. The bite was shallow. The number was a hair off in shape. I did not write fake. I wrote weak.

"Now the part where we slow our hearts," I said. "We go to comps."

I pulled the laptop under the lamp and opened my saved searches. Sales closed, not listed. Condition flagged with notes, not adjectives. I passed over dreamers with a single photo and a price that pretends dust can pay a mortgage. I clicked on two auctions from the last six months that showed straight spines, true decks, and honest colophons. I read the line about the board cloth fading and the light bump to a corner, proof of life. I wrote those closing prices on the card without flinching and drew a thin line under them. Then I opened two dealer records that sold off platform, wrote those prices with a tilde to mark the uncertainty, and underlined the line where the dealer mentioned sending macro shots on request. Dealers who say that know their job.

"And now we add the suspect column," I said. "We look at what falls short."

She watched while I typed a short line to an old foreman who knows this press the way sailors know a bell. I attached the macro of the colophon dots and wrote him the one sentence he needs. Alignment reads off by half a dot. Confirm or tell me I need sleep. I sent the file and marked the card with a small square that means a response is in flight.

I had not invited Seth. He arrived anyway, the way rain does when you forgot the tarp. He leaned in the doorway with a grin he did not earn and checked the room for a crowd he did not deserve.

"I knew you would drag this out," he said, friendly on the surface, sand under the teeth. "How many tabs open so far. Twelve. Twenty."

"Four," I said. "Enough."

He slid in and palmed his phone on the glass with the screen bright. The same title looked back at us. Same jacket. Different spine stamp. His photo had been taken on a kitchen table with a bowl of oranges in the corner and a hand I did not know hovering near the gutter, ring on the right. The stamp sat a fraction lower and bit deeper than ours. The metadata string ran across the top like an address label that refused to peel off. Yesterday, ten minutes before the time Daria's invite listed for her club.

He made a show of pinching the image to zoom. "See where the cloth pulls a whisper at the joint," he said. "That is what you want. Yours does not have it."

"You sent this to Talia yesterday," I said.

"She asked me for help," he said.

"She brought the box to me," I said. "We are helping."

FIRST EDITIONS AND FINAL WORDS

He pointed at the column where I had written weak next to spine stamp. "You already know what I know," he said. "Why slow walk what we all see. Buyers are awake right now. This hour is good. By afternoon someone else will fill their basket with a safer item."

"We are not a basket," I said. "We are a shop."

He ignored that and hooked his thumb into his belt like a foreman about to tell a crowd to lift together. "The market does not wait for tea," he said. "You consign here, you consign your shot at a clean payday. I am offering cash. No percentage. No pageantry. I can wire by lunch."

Talia looked at me and then at him. She held her breath for a second and then let it go through her teeth.

"What is your number," she asked.

He named a number that knew exactly how to charm a person who has a tuition invoice in a folder that lives under a pillow. I did not blink. A lowball dressed like a favor smells like apples left in a drawer.

"Show your math," I said. "Closed sales, not the dream you woke up with."

"Trade secret," he said. He tapped his temple and smiled.

"I sleep fine without that secret," I said. "If you need to go to the diner to keep your coffee appointment, you should go. We are pricing against facts."

He rolled his eyes so hard I worried for his optic nerves, then pivoted to Talia with one last lean. "I like to see young people win," he said. "Old shops like to watch them learn."

"Old shops keep them from getting robbed," I said.

He pocketed the phone and planted a finger on the cradle lid as if he planned to press. I put my hand on the other side. He saw the angle and withdrew. He grinned again, split like a paper cut.

"Have it your way," he said. "Watch for forgeries. They are everywhere this week. The last thing you want is to be the shop that blessed a fake."

"Blessings are from the church down the block," I said. "We offer receipts."

He left with the kind of shrug people practice in gym mirrors when they need a whole room to register that they are far above pettiness. The bell rang the sound of a lid set down a touch harder than needed. Peppermint opened one eye, dismissed the weather, and went back to being a comma.

"Is his number good," Talia asked, quiet.

"For the book in his photo with the deeper stamp, if the colophon passes," I said. "Not for this one."

I slipped on gloves again, turned the page to thirteen, and showed her the tiny wobble Theo would admire in a way that means trouble. "This edge has been shaved," I said. "One light pass to make a deckle read cleaner for a hurried eye. It hurts value. It also tells us a hand touched this with intent."

"If it is fake, is anything in this box real," she asked.

"The box is not a sentence," I said. "It is chapters. Some are clean. Some are messy. Some belong in the case, some on the front table with a sticker that says good reading for Wednesday."

She laughed once, short, a sound that shook out some of the fear.

"Now the part where we put numbers on paper," I said.

I wrote a provisional floor and ceiling for three titles that looked straight, based on comps with honest photos and notes. I slid those cards to the left. I wrote a provisional number with a low ceiling for our suspect and slid it to the right. I wrote a third number, zero, and circled it, because that is what you write when your gut says hold. Then I unlocked the small cabinet under the counter and took out the consignment folder with the clean forms and the small flags that mark clauses people skip and regret.

I walked her through it. Percentage split, time frame, publicity opt in or out, return conditions, insurance while on premises, transport chain if we send a book to an outside lab, dispute path that keeps people from using my counter as a stage. I read every clause out loud and asked for a nod on each one. Miss Dotty drifted back to the window with a paperback and pretended to read while she listened. Peppermint kneaded the sill. People underestimate the way a cat can hold a room together.

"Do you like math," Talia asked, head tilted.

"I like order," I said. "Math is one way to be fair. Paper is another. I keep both where I can find them."

She signed the form with a hand that still trembled and then steadied. She checked the box that said no publicity, because there are people in this town who stage kindness for social media and she has no patience left for empty applause. I initialed the chain clause twice because the last thing I want is a man like Seth telling someone I let their box go on a ride with a stranger.

We tagged each title with its intake number and a short checklist of points to confirm. Rafi brought a tray with three waters and two lemon cookies because sugar helps in rooms where people stare at paper a long time. He set one cookie next to Peppermint, who sniffed it like a scholar and turned away. He prefers salmon. He is not wrong.

The email ping came back from the foreman at the press before I had time to refill my pencil. He wrote one line that held exactly enough.

Your macro shows offset on the dots, not a true bite. Our grid rides half a dot left on that year, not right. Ink density is wrong. Do not bless it.

I turned the screen so Talia could read it. She closed her eyes, opened them, and nodded like a person who has watched a doctor write down a word that is not the word you wanted and decided to keep breathing anyway.

"Okay," she said. "Okay. So that one is a loss."

"It is information," I said. "Information makes the next decision cleaner."

"I wanted clean money," she said.

"You will get clean money from the others," I said. "This one is a lesson we will turn into a safety talk for customers who come in asking why their uncle's book is worth an alarming number. Lessons can be useful if we pay them once and not twice."

She touched the edge of the cradle and then took her hand back as if she had touched a stove. "I did not do this," she said, to the air, to herself, to the floor.

"I know," I said.

We went through two more titles, both midlist from the right decade with edges that felt like proper air and boards that felt like cloth, not plastic that wants to be cloth. I wrote prices we both could live with. I slid those books into the case with a small smile. A case with new inventory makes a room stand taller.

Then I pulled out a second suspect from the crate, the one that had read burnished. I set it under the lamp and took a small breath I kept when the room was empty. You can hear your own thinking if you keep your breath steady. I turned the board and caught the catch. A soft sheen where no sheen should live. Someone had decided a gloss would read as youth. Youth is valued by shoppers who do not know how paper grows up. I wrote burnish in the points column and moved on. I would send this one to Theo for a gentle touch with a clean cloth and a safe solvent handshake if he agreed there was no danger. If there was danger, back it went to the box with a label that said hold for conversation.

Miss Dotty set her paperback face down, a thing she almost never does, and folded her hands on the edge of the counter. "Children will be bringing macaroni art to graduations if you let men like that run rooms," she said, chin toward the door where Seth had disappeared. "Teach the girl to hold a line. The town will thank you later."

"Help me, then," I said. "Tell me what you see when you look at this spine."

She slid her glasses down and peered at the presswork. "Letterforms that were cut by someone who did not like the letter R," she said. "A lightness on the tail that tells me the punch was not deep enough. And a confidence I would like to borrow. Whoever did this knew they could get away with it if they moved fast. Slow them down."

I wrote slow them down in small letters in the corner of the card and put a box around it. I like a reminder in my own hand to do what I already know.

The phone buzzed with a message. Seth again. You can lock the box here or you can let the girl eat. Time on this one will not be kind. I put the phone face down and wrote another line in the chain column to mark the contact with a time stamp. Contact with picker, pressure language logged. If anyone ever asks what kind of pressure, I will print that text and tape it to my answer.

I turned back to Talia. "Here is what I propose," I said. "We consign the safe titles today, price them fair, and put them in the case before lunch. We hold the suspect for lab notes and a side by side with a known real copy from the press foreman's file. We do not touch the money until the facts have the weight we like. In the meantime, I will email three buyers who like clean midlist and pay on time. We aim for two sales this week. The third can sit until the weekend. If all goes well, your room will smell like new paint by Thursday."

She stared at the two safe titles in the case, then at the suspect on the cradle. She pressed her lips together in a thin straight line, not angry, not afraid, a line that said she had made a decision and would keep it.

"Consign here," she said. "I want a receipt I can show my aunt where her name is spelled right and the dates match what the sun thinks it is. I want a person who will answer the phone. I want to learn what a deckle is without wanting to cry."

"Done," I said.

She signed the last flag in the form, the one that says you have read the whole thing and still plan to do this. I handed her the copy and clipped ours into the drawer with the clean copy of our insurance rider. I printed two barcode stickers, one for each safe title, and pressed them to the mylar sleeves. I wrote pending in red on the suspect's tag and taped the bag shut.

As I stood to slide the suspect into the hold cabinet, the bell chimed and Seth appeared again with a shrug and a grin that tried to read like I am not here to bother you. He put his phone away this time and set both hands on the counter like a man about to pray.

"Make sure you test the colophon," he said. "I have heard about a rash of fakes with print that leans a half dot the wrong way. You do not want to bless that."

"We do not bless anything," I said. "We check. We checked. Thank you."

He watched my hands put the suspect in the cabinet. He watched the key turn. He watched me pocket the key before he could suggest a new path for it.

"Suit yourself," he said. He paused, studied Talia's face, then added in a tone he thought could pass as gentle, "There are sharks at this beach. I hope your life jacket is not made of paper."

"Paper floats if you fold it right," she said. "I am folding it here."

He held my eye for one second longer than manners allow, nodded, and left. The bell told the room he had gone. Peppermint lifted his head and sent him off with a blink that said nothing and everything.

I slid the safe titles into the front of the case. Glass makes a satisfying hush when it closes on a new thing you trust. I printed clean shelf cards with short notes. First printing, honest edge, jacket bright, no chips. Priced fair. No adjectives that sell dreams. Facts that sell to readers who respect their own eyes.

"Lunch on me," Miss Dotty said, half to Peppermint, half to the air. "Soup travels well."

"Tomato," I said. "And if the bread is warm, we will not

complain."

She tipped her hat at Talia, tucked the paperback under her arm, and left with a gait that said she would be back with a paper bag that contained a steadying agent.

I took a photo of the case for our records and emailed a buyer who has never returned a package and never asked me to lie on an invoice. I wrote the line I always write him. Two clean arrivals today. Notes attached. First hold on you for forty minutes. He tends to answer in twelve. He did it in eight, a single yes for one of the midlist, and a keep me posted on the second. I sent an invoice and copied Talia. I like people to see what moves and how.

We stood for a moment in a rare quiet. Peppermint stretched, reached his paw into the air as if he had grabbed the last stray worry, and then relaxed.

Talia folded her copy of the form into her bag and zipped it like sealing a letter. "Thank you," she said. "For not letting him take the box and for not letting me be stupid in public."

"You were not stupid," I said. "You were scared. Scared people either run or lean. You leaned."

She smiled the way people do when they still do not believe good things but are willing to let them near.

"Now we ring the sale," I said. "Small money first. Big money later. That is how roofs get paid for."

The bell chimed a soft hello as a pair of regulars wandered in, eyes on the case, hands already reaching for their wallets in the casual way people buy themselves a kind day. I looked at the cradle, at the hold cabinet, at the case with its bright cards, and at the column on my working sheet that reads proof. The macro sat in the file, the foreman's one line in my inbox, the deckle wobble under my notes, the spines split between the photo and the board in front of me. The room felt like a ledger where every number had started to balance.

"Okay," Talia said, shoulders lower, voice clear. "We consign."

She offered her hand, dry and firm. I took it. A deal is not real until two people touch it. We touched it. Peppermint approved with a small sigh that sounded like a stamp.

Seth's warning about forgeries hung in the doorway like fog. I wrote it on the card where it belonged, not as prophecy, as context. Then I slid the card under the lamp, squared the corners so they sat inside the beam, and turned to the next task.

CHAPTER 3

Colophon Doubt

I set the loupe on the counter like a small oath. The rare nook hums at a low, steady note. Good paper likes the same sort of air my plants prefer. Dry. Predictable. The task lamp throws a clean circle across the cloth mat. Inside that circle sits the book that wants to be a windfall.

Peppermint lifts his head from the sill and studies me the way he studies moths. Tail tip flick, ears forward. Talia hovers near the end of the counter with her hand on the strap of her bag, knuckles pale. Miss Dotty Bell inches closer with a paperback in her palm and a hat that looks older than the case behind me. She is browsing, which for her means waiting until I give the street a show worth watching.

"Ready," I say to the room. It helps no one and still helps everyone.

I slide the cradle into place. The boards creak a breath as I ease the weight onto the gutter. Gloves on. Wrist loose. I draw the loupe down and bring the colophon to the center of the light. The mark looks right from an arm's length. The way a smile looks right from across a street. Up close it asks for questions.

Dot grids behave like people. They have habits. Each press carries a bias that shows up as a tiny lean. It repeats across years. Foremen pass it to apprentices without saying a word. I have a box in the back with sample sheets that show that lean in quiet rows. The book on the mat wants to fake that habit and fakes it with confidence.

I lower my eye to the loupe. The circle swallows the world until only dots and fibers remain. The grid sits a half step off its lineage. The low row leans right. The true mark for this press leans left, a shy shift you only see when a lens stops pretending. The ink tells on itself too. Letterpress ink has a way of pooling where metal kisses paper. A rim, a slight well, a softness at the edge where force met fiber and the fiber took the kiss. Offset wants even coverage. It gives you rain on glass. Smooth, clean, even.

"Talk to me," Miss Dotty says, not quite a command, not quite a plea.

"Half step misaligned," I say. "Ink density tells a smooth story. Too smooth. Wrong for a bite. Right for a roll."

Talia breathes out through her nose and steadies herself on the mat with two fingers. "Is misaligned always a lie," she asks.

"No," I say. "But this press runs left on this year. This runs right by a hair. A hair matters when money perches on that hair."

I set the loupe down and slide the mark under a metric rule I use for photographs. The rule gives the shot a known scale so the camera can read truth later. I angle the lens, press the shutter, and capture the corner where the dots drift. I take a second shot to catch the ink edge. I write the time on a card and tuck it under the lens for the next frame. Chain of custody looks fussy until someone calls from a conference table and asks which minute matters.

Peppermint hops to the chair that faces the counter and watches the lens blink. He trills once, a small sound that gives the moment a hinge. He smells vinegar where I smell ink. He always smells what I miss first.

Miss Dotty leans in. "That press never looked like that," she says. She taps the edge of the page with her cane tip, careful not to touch. "See where the bottom row lands. See how the right side floats. Someone tried to copy a habit and made a choice that no apprentice from that shop would make, not even on a Wednesday when the rain kept the trucks from loading on time."

Her voice is dry and gentle and thin as rice paper. It also cuts. Talia swallows. She does not speak. I lift the book a fraction and angle the page to catch the light across the ink. Relief should show at this angle if the plate pressed hard enough. The surface stays flat. No lift. No burr.

I move the loupe across the colophon and count fibers. Fibers tell the year of a sheet like rings tell the age of a tree. This stock feels right in weight and wrong in surface. A burnish sits over the board cloth that carries into the endpaper. Someone smoothed what should stay honest. I slide a fingernail along the edge and stop when the glove reminds me where my nail ends and the page begins.

Talia points at the grid, cautious. "You said left for the real ones," she says.

"Left by a hint," I say. "This goes right by a hint. Also, look at the dots on the outer column. Each one has a halo instead of a bruise. It reads like offset. No bruise, no squeeze, no small ridge. Letterpress leaves a rim you can catch in the wrong light."

"Can light be wrong," she asks, trying for humor and landing close.

"Any light that flatters a lie," I say. "This circle does not flatter."

She smiles despite herself. Miss Dotty smiles too and slides her paperback across the counter as a headrest for her wrists. The paperback is a romance with a cover that makes no promise it does not keep. Dotty does this when a hard truth needs soft hands. She lets a mass market back a rare point.

I bring out a control. An old board from the same press, different book, same year. I keep it in a sleeve with a red stripe that tells me this is not to sell, not to loan, not to lose. The grid on the control leans left. The dots show a thin rim when you tilt the page and squint. Ink pools where a metal kiss pressed down. I put the two marks side by side and let the lamp do all the talking.

Talia's eyes widen. "I see it," she says. Relief and grief ride the same tone when a person sees and can no longer pretend not to. "I wanted not to see it," she adds.

"That is why I put the control out," I say. "So we do not have to fight memory."

I photograph both colophons with the metric rule. One shot wide. One shot tight. I write a small ID on a white card with a pencil. I do not trust my memory to hold a number while Rafi asks me about creamers or Peppermint breaks up a fight with a dust bunny under Romance.

Miss Dotty watches my hands. "Do you remember the atlas forgery from three winters back," she asks me.

"I do," I say. "Same confidence. Different tool marks."

She nods. "Confidence is the hardest finish to sand off," she says. "Ink lifts. Glue scrapes. Confidence lingers."

I set the book flat and let the handles on the cradle hold the boards. I track the ink across the colophon with a low angle penlight and look for squeeze. The edge stays tidy. A machine passed a kiss over this spot. It did not press like a plate.

Talia shifts on her feet. "So whoever made this changed a small thing about a tiny row of dots and thought the price would follow," she says.

"That or they do not know the map," I say. "Fakes love clean ideas. Real prints love habits. Habits betray a shop when a faker forgets he is imitating a person and not a logo."

She drags one finger across her cup of water and looks at the circle it leaves. "I can live with a page out of order," she says. "I can live with a bruise on a jacket. This feels like someone wrote on my aunt's check with a crayon and told me not to mind the color."

Miss Dotty laughs under her breath. "That is right," she says.

The bell at the door rings a small, polite hello. A pair of teachers from the school down the block wander in, head straight for the case, and lean on each other the way friends do when they share a budget and a taste. I raise a hand and they wave. They know when the circle of light means wait.

I tip the book to check for emboss. The press stamp at the rear board sits tight and shallow. Another small tell. The shop that printed this title bit deeper that year. Not a gouge. A confidence of touch. This reads shy.

"Walk me through letterpress again," Talia says. "I want to be able to explain this without sounding like I learned it ten minutes ago."

"Plates with type and rules," I say. "Ink on the raised parts. Paper meets plate with force and kisses back. The kiss leaves a rim where ink pools at the edge of pressure. You can feel a hint of it under a finger if your hand listens. Offset uses plates and blankets with a dance between cylinders. Ink travels to a rubber blanket. The blanket transfers the image to the paper with pressure that spreads. You get smooth, even fields and dots without rims. When a faker uses offset to fake a bite, a loupe hears the lie."

"Why would anyone fake a little mark in the back of the book," she asks.

"Because the little mark pulls big money toward the front," I say.

She nods and squares her shoulders. "Okay," she says. "I can repeat that back if I sleep once."

"You will," I say. "Not yet."

I slide the loupe to her and let her look through. She peers like a jeweler checking a ring in a parking lot. She pulls back. She looks again. A third look lands. She handles the lens better on the third pass and stops pressing her brow to the rim. People learn lenses the way they learn seasickness. Slowly. Then all at once.

"Half step," she says. "Right, not left."

"Good," I say.

"And too even," she says.

"Yes," I say.

She bites her lip. "If someone did this in town, I am going to have a problem not saying words my grandmother tried to teach me not to say in front of cash drawers," she says.

"Save them for the alley," I say.

Peppermint stands and drops to the counter with the soft thud of a book set down in a quiet room. He tiptoes to the cradle and noses the edge of the sleeve. I block with my palm and he decides the metric rule needs warming instead. He lays across it and pretends to be a paperweight.

The foreman at the press is a practical man who answers emails in one line if he likes you and in no lines if he does not. I type the subject line. Colophon dot drift, confirm bias and density for your year. I attach the macro with the scale and the control shot. I do not send questions before I send proof. People who work with machines prefer evidence to feelings.

While the message warms up in the outbox, I pull out a reference book from the case. Not a coffee table heavy thing. A thin press history by a person who counted dots for a living. It has a chapter on the local shop and a table that lists known shifts in templates from one maintenance cycle to the next. I run my finger down the column and find the year. A small note says lean left on low row after winter service. Clean stamp on rear board once the pressman stopped smoking near the blanket. The note makes me feel seen by strangers I will never meet.

I show Talia the page and the note. "It is not only me," I say.

"Happy to blame a table," she says.

The teachers leave the case with a pair of used hardcovers and a romance I know Dotty read twice and bought a third time for the cover. Rafi rings them up and slides bookmarks across the counter with the reflex of a man who knows people lose them within an hour. The bell rings and the room settles again.

I measure the size of the stamp impression with the metric rule and write the reading down. I do the same for the control. Numbers hush a fight before it starts. I write the difference in blunt digits, not in adjectives. Blunt digits do not get sued.

"Where do we go from here," Talia asks.

"Bag a macro," I say. "Tag the book. Lock the cabinet. Note the time. Then we go to Theo with the deckle. After that we ask questions that have names on them, not theories."

She nods. "Names like Walter," she says. "The printer with the garage."

"Names like that," I say.

She leans into the counter. "He showed up at the house once with a toolbox," she says. "Said he wanted to look at an old pamphlet my aunt said she had. He stayed an hour and left with a small envelope he said she gave him. She told me later she had not found the pamphlet after all."

I write this down in the margin of the card. Small envelope, Walter, toolbox. People like to call anything with a hinge a toolbox. The word covers a lot of sins.

"Who else handled the book before it reached me," I ask.

"Seth," she says. "He touched the jacket when he took the picture. He touched the spine when he told me not to breathe near it. He told me a soft deckle is a sign of quality. He said that part out loud. Then I watched a video and felt stupid."

"You are not stupid," I say.

She breathes. "I am learning to see," she says.

Miss Dotty beams. "Good sentence," she says.

I bag the macro print with a label that includes the time, my initials, and the intake number. I slip it into a sleeve with a zip that seals flat. I take two more shots to catch the texture of the ink at a longer angle. I hold my breath for the second shot because the coffee machine hisses at the wrong moment.

Peppermint hears it too and flicks an ear. The shot lands clean.

I print the macros on the small photo printer I keep for mornings like this. The paper curls as it comes out. I flatten it under the metric rule, which annoys Peppermint. He swats the edge, then retreats with dignity intact.

"Do you ever feel like the whole town watches your hands," Talia asks.

"Yes," I say. "It makes me pour tea slower."

"Tea is not helping right now," she says.

"Soup will," Miss Dotty says from the doorway where she now stands with a white paper sack. She had slipped out while we counted dots and returned with warmth. "Tomato and a heel of bread. I paid. You will eat."

She sets the bag on the far corner, away from the circle of light. Steam slips out when I open it. The smell settles into the room and edges the anxiety. Talia takes the cup I offer and holds it like a scrying bowl. She does not drink yet. She waits for the next line in this small play.

I choose a red tag from the stack and print pending across the top. I write a short list in the box below the line. Colophon drift right. Ink too even. Rear stamp shallow. Deckle shave suspected. Macro filed. Control compared. I sign and date. I tape the tag to the mylar and close the sleeve with a gentle press that clicks when the zip finds home.

"Say it out loud," Miss Dotty says.

"Pending," I say. "Hold until confirmation from press foreman. No price quote. No show."

Talia breathes out as if she had been holding a plank over a pool. She takes a sip of soup and a bite of bread and her shoulders drop. She can hear the plan now. Plans calm.

I slide the book into the hold cabinet. The hinge sighs. The lock clicks. I pocket the key and write its place on the peg board behind the desk. I do this even when memory says I do not need to. Memory has lied to me before, mostly on days when the shop is full and my phone will not stop flashing at the corner of my sight.

Peppermint jumps from the counter and lands by the hold cabinet with a soft thump. He presses his cheek to the wood. He likes the vibration of the fan. I tell myself this guard routine is intentional and not indulgent. He blinks and proves me wrong.

He presses his cheek to the wood, then blinks at me as if to ask what comes next. I answer by doing the job. I pull a red tag from the stack and print PENDING in block letters. I note the time, the intake number, and the colophon drift. I sign and date. The pen lifts clean. No flourish.

The macro prints slide from the tray still warm. I label each with the scale mark and my initials and slip them into a sleeve. The zipper closes with a neat click. I record the entry on the chain card and tuck the card in front.

The book goes into the hold cabinet. The hinge sighs. The lock turns. I pocket the key and write its hook on the peg board for later. Rafi checks my face again. I give him the same small nod. We are good.

Talia watches my hands and lets out a steady breath. "So we wait," she says.

"We wait with proof," I say.

I set the sleeve in the evidence bin and tape the red tag to the mylar. Then I say it for the room.

"Macro bagged. Book tagged pending."

The task lamp hums. The facts hold. We move to the next step.

CHAPTER 4

Deckle Shave

Theo had the bindery bench cleared before I reached it. Clean felt on the surface, bone folders in a fan at the top right, two microfibre cloths folded into squares, and a small bin labeled edges. The bench light is a narrow bar that throws a cool line across paper. It is merciless in all the ways I like.

Peppermint followed us in with the stride of a cat who owns floor plans. He leapt to the stool, judged the height, then chose the radiator shelf instead and stretched long enough to touch both brackets. Talia stood across from me with her palms flat on the bench. She watched the book as if it might jump.

Theo slid on cotton gloves and did not speak. He never does during the first minute. He listens with his fingertips. He set the suspect on the cradle, adjusted the straps without looking at them, and let the board rest. He passed his right index finger along the fore-edge, slow, not pressing, the way a reader strokes a ribbon when a chapter ends.

"Too smooth," he said.

I felt the knot in my shoulders approve. "Say where," I said.

"From head to foot," he said. "More at the center. The rise and fall you expect on a deckle is muted. The feather that should catch a nail has been taught manners it never had."

He tilted the book and sighted down the edge. Light skated across the paper and showed the faint rhythm a hand-formed sheet wears when it dries. Here and there that rhythm broke for a line that whispered machine, not vat. That alone would not be a hanging offense for this title. But the edge read wrong. Deckles are born with a rind that catches and releases as you move. This one wanted to slide.

"How would someone smooth it," Talia asked, soft.

Theo reached for the small tray of tools and chose a hobby blade with a new edge. He held it up so the light caught the metal. No flourish. No classroom tone. "One light pass like this," he said. He took a scrap of rag paper from the bin, let it hang from the clamp, and drew the blade along the edge with the faintest pressure. The curl that lifted from the sheet was almost nothing, a ghost of white that drifted into his glove. He laid the trimmed scrap next to an untrimmed piece and let Talia touch both.

"The trimmed one slides," she said.

He nodded once. "People shave because a ragged deckle can read like neglect to a browser who knows price tags and not papermills. If your goal is to fool a casual eye, you shave. If your goal is to keep value, you leave what the vat gave you."

He turned to the suspect and opened to page thirteen. Fingers under the board, wrist straight, movement tidy. He held the fore-edge to the light again, then passed the pad of his thumb along a half inch in the lower third.

"Here," he said. "A catch."

I leaned in and saw it. Not a gouge. Not a tear. A micro flat where the blade had wobbled and met itself a second longer than planned. I lifted the loupe and pulled the edge into the circle. The wobble bloomed into a tiny plateau with a hairline nick running perpendicular to the cut. The kind of mark a hand leaves when a phone buzzes in a pocket at the wrong moment.

"Photograph," I said.

He pivoted the edge under the task bar so the light grazed it and handed me the metric rule. I set the rule across the margin, lining the zero at the plateau, and took the shot. One vertical, one rotated, then one pulled back to show the location on the page. I wrote page 13 lower third, edge flat, and the time, then slipped a note card beneath the edge for the final frame. Chain does not keep you from being wrong. It keeps you from being lazy.

Talia breathed out like she had been holding a plank. "What does that do to value," she asked.

"On a clean copy, a trimmed edge can turn a top number into a middle number," I said. "On a copy with other questions, it turns the number into a conversation, sometimes with a refund attached."

She nodded. "And it tells us someone held a blade in this house," she said.

"This town," Theo said. He did not look up from the edge. He moved three leaves forward and ran his index finger along the fore-edge again. "The pass is not even. Whoever shaved did not use a guide. Hobby tool, not the guillotine at a bindery. I would bet on a tabletop and a video tutorial."

He set the blade back in its tray like it had asked to sit. He reached for a sheet of scrap and demonstrated a second time, lighter, to show how a careful hand would avoid a plateau. The curl lifted and fell as weightless as onion skin. He put both trimmed scraps under the bar and let the light compare them.

"Can you fix it," Talia asked.

"We can ease a gloss and chair a corner back into truth," he said. "We cannot put rind back where it was shaved. You can dress a wound. You cannot give the paper its birth again."

Her mouth quirked at that. "No magic," she said.

"No magic," he said.

He moved to the head edge and checked the cut there. The top read closer to correct, but at the center another faint flat lived two leaves back. He logged it with a sticky flag and a pencil mark on our worksheet. He keeps a grid for these inspections. Columns for head, fore, foot. Rows for obvious issues and notes. When Theo hands you a worksheet you can taste the hour it cost him to build the template.

"Turn it," I said.

He closed to the title spread and lifted the fore-edge, then turned the book in place so the light changed. The plateau at thirteen looked larger in this angle. I took a second macro, then a third. Peppermint sat up on the radiator shelf, focused on the curl as if it were a moth only he could see.

"You have done this before," Talia said to Theo.

"People watch videos and want their book to look new," he said. "They bring me the patient after they practice. The debt lands on my bench. I tell them what I tell everyone. Clean is fine. Honest is better."

He picked up the hobby blade and handed it to Talia across his palm. "Weight," he said. She set her fingers on it like it might burn.

"Light," she said.

"Which makes you think it cannot hurt," he said. "Then it does."

She placed it back as if it belonged to someone else and wiped her palm on her jeans. "If my aunt did not do this, who did," she asked.

"That is the question for the hour," I said.

Theo opened to thirteen again, flagged the flat, then stepped through six more leaves with the rhythm of a person counting a deck that has a queen missing. He found two faint rubs where the blade caught pith and moved on. He found a gloss on the fore-edge near page seventy and tapped it. "Handling with lotion," he said. "Small smear, not a sin."

He closed, rested his palms on the bench for a count of five, then lifted the book with both hands and settled it back into the evidence sleeve. He sealed the zip, pressed the line flat, and wrote a line on the chain card in his careful block letters. Fore-edge shave visible, page 13 flat. Photos filed. Theo M. Then he gave me the sleeve.

I wrote the same note on my working sheet and added a short sentence to the points column. Edge pass uneven, likely hand cut, hobby blade. I drew a small box around page 13 and underlined it. I will want to show that plateau beside the colophon drift for anyone who asks why my tone has changed about this copy.

Talia watched my pencil. "What does page thirteen tell you," she asked.

"I keep a habit of writing the first hard fact in a place I can find at speed," I said. "Thirteen can be any number. It is where my eye will land first when we brief."

She nodded again. Theo slid the blade back into its case and wiped the bench with the heel of his hand, a tiny motion that tells me a thought stuck to him.

"Say it," I said.

"Someone learned on this copy," he said. "The hand had confidence before skill. That puts a person with tools near your aunt and near a place where watching a lot of short videos passes for practice."

"The club," I said.

"The club," he said.

Talia's face went from tight to tired. "Daria," she said.

"Not only," I said. "People bring blades to rooms when they want attention. Daria is a room that sells attention by the yard."

Theo pulled a small scale from the drawer and weighed the curl he had trimmed from the scrap. He wrote the number on his worksheet, though there is no need. He likes numbers. They keep him from arguing with his hands. He slid the curl into a glassine envelope, labeled it scrap test, and tucked it under the evidence sleeve for the book, not because it belongs to this case but because it helps the story travel.

"Do you want a solvent pass on the board gloss," he asked me.

"Not yet," I said. "I want to show it as we found it. When the questions have names, we can ask if a lift helps."

He nodded and put the solvent back on the top shelf. He has learned where my brakes live and leaves them on.

Peppermint dropped from the shelf and padded to the bin labeled edges. He sat beside it like a sentry and flicked his tail. Theo reached down, lifted the lid, and let him look in as if the cat had the right. Peppermint sniffed the rag paper and withdrew with dignity. He prefers linen.

I photographed the bench sheet with the flags for our file, then took a close shot of the blade nick and the plateau from a second angle. I wrote the time on the card and tucked it into the photo frame for the last shot. I like one picture that proves when as well as what.

"Write your note," Theo said.

He knows my habits as well as I know his. I pulled the small red notebook from my apron and wrote the line I would want if the printer foreman calls while I am pouring tea for a customer with a bag of poetry. Page 13 flat from blade wobble, fore-edge shave, hand pass without guide, hobby blade weight. Underneath I added one more sentence because it matters here. Learn on scrap, not on a life.

Talia read the last line and smiled without any humor. "I might frame that," she said.

"Do," I said.

She tucked her hair behind her ear. "I should have known," she said. "The spine stamp and the deckle and the ink. It feels like I walked through the house and missed the cat on the stairs."

"You are here now," I said. "This is where we stop missing."

Theo slipped off the gloves and washed his hands at the small sink. He folded the cotton and put them in the bin that lives under the bench. He dries his hands with the second cloth, wipes the bar light with the corner, and nods to show the bench is ready for the next hour.

I sealed the sleeve, taped on a small flag for easy pull, and wrote PENDING DECKLE on the red tag under the colophon note. The letters looked a shade sharper than they had an hour ago. Paper talks to ink. Ink listens.

"Who brought the blade near these pages," I said, not loud, not soft. I looked at Talia.

She flinched at the question, not at the tone. "Seth walked the box into the living room the first day," she said. "He took the top copy out and held it without asking. He does that. He said the deckle was handsome. He handed it to Daria when she came by that night to talk about a club teaser. She had a tote with enamel pins and a phone that never sleeps. She asked if she could take one photo and then took nine. She left with the tote heavier than she came with. I did not see a blade. I was in the kitchen with my aunt and a stack of paper plates, trying to make the house look like a place that could host people."

Theo held my eye without moving his head. Daria and a heavier tote. Page thirteen and a wobble. The colophon drift and the even ink. A pattern was writing itself in the air.

I logged the wobble on the chain card, signed my initials, and put the book back into the hold cabinet. The key turned with a click that sounded like a period.

"Good," I said. "Now we ask more questions, one at a time."

Peppermint rubbed his cheek along the lower drawer and made a small sound that lives somewhere between a purr and a note. He likes when the plan is simple.

"Who showed you the lot first, Talia," I said. "Name, not role."

She met my eyes and did not look away. "Daria," she said. "She knocked before Seth. She saw the boxes through the front window and called it fate. I called it Tuesday."

CHAPTER 5

Seller Missing

Talia rang twice before my phone finished the first vibration. I answered on the third tone and heard breath before words, the kind of breath you take when a plan falls out of your hands.

"She is not home," she said. "Her car is out front. Lights in the kitchen. Keys on the hook."

"Tell me where you are," I said.

"In the foyer," she said. "I unlocked the door with the spare under the frog planter. I called out. Nothing."

"Step outside," I said. "Wait on the porch. I am on my way. Do not touch the counters. Do not wander."

"I can do that," she said, and hung up.

I locked the hold cabinet, pocketed the key, and told Rafi that we had a welfare check. He knows the tone for that. He slid me a pen and the small evidence notebook without speaking and nodded at Peppermint, who had already stepped down from the radiator shelf and taken the aisle with the purposeful walk he saves for trouble.

The street held its usual Saturday rhythm. Coffee cups. Strollers. A bike bell that thought it was a song. I cut right at the florist and left at the deli with the blue awning and drove two blocks past the estate. I parked out of sight and walked back so I could see the front windows before I came within earshot.

The house was a neat box with green trim and a porch that begged for cooler weather. The welcome mat read Hello in a font that had tried too hard to be kind. Talia stood near the banister, one hand on the post and the other wrapped tight around her phone. She wore the expression everyone wears when a house that should stop trouble decides to let it in.

"Talk me through what you saw," I said, stepping up. "Start at the gate."

"I came straight from your shop," she said. "I should have texted first. I did not. The front door was locked. No answer when I called. I walked around. The back gate latch had paint chips under it like someone fussed with the hinge. I know that door. It sticks when the air gets wet. I came back to the front, lifted the frog, and used the spare. I called her name three times from the railing. Nothing. I stepped in and I saw the keys on the hook where she always leaves them. I walked to the kitchen doorway and saw a mug on the counter with a ring and the tea bag tag tucked under. I did not touch the mug. I walked back and called you."

"You did fine," I said. "Stand with me. We go one step at a time."

We stood on the threshold long enough to hear the house breathe. Houses have their own version of a chest. Radiators sigh. Refrigerators hum. Old wood talks to itself. The wrong sound in that chorus is a heavy thing. I listened for movement and heard none.

"Announce," I said. "Loud enough to reach the hallway."

Talia lifted her chin. "Aunt Mara, it's Talia," she called. "We are here. Liora is with me."

Silence sat down again. I took a photo of the doormat and the threshold, then the key hook inside the door with the keys in place. Front door, locked when we arrived, spare used, keys on hook, photo taken, time noted. I wrote it in the small book with the calm script that keeps my hand honest.

We stepped inside together. The foyer smelled like lemon oil and paper. A drop-leaf table held a bowl for mail and a small brass cat with chipped paint on one ear. A light on the far end of the hall fought the daylight and lost. I put a glove on my right hand and used the back of my knuckle to nudge open the kitchen door. The mug sat near the sink. The tag showed an orange blend from the grocer with the chalkboard sign outside.

"Look at the counter," I said.

Talia leaned as far as the doorframe and stopped. "Clean," she said. "No crumbs. No breakage. She hates a mess more than bills."

I took a photo of the mug and the tag, then one of the calendar on the side of the fridge where she wrote book club at Daria's in a tight hand. The day before was marked with a star and the word bring shortbread. I opened the drawer near the refrigerator with the edge of my glove. Spoons. Clips. A small pad with a shopping list that included sugar, not sugar free, underlined twice. That line mattered more than I liked.

We went room by room with the method I use when I think I know what I will find and do not want to be wrong. Study first. Chair pushed in. Lamp off. A stack of estate forms with sticky notes on names. The top sheet held a phone photo of a book with a spine stamp that did not match the copy in my cabinet. I photographed the photo on the form and the form itself and wrote the time.

Bedroom. Bed made. Nightstand with a paperback and a bookmark that read Take your time. The closet door stood open with a set of flats on the floor that matched the ghost of dust on the front steps. They had not moved since yesterday. The bathroom held a towel folded on the rack and a toothbrush dry enough to tell me no one brushed here in the last hour.

Back door next. We moved as a pair, not because I needed help with the hinge but because people do better when they share the line. The latch showed the paint chip Talia mentioned. I photographed the chip and the strike plate and the gap where humid wood meets a frame built by a person who never met August.

The porch faced a fence that backed into a narrow lane I would not call an alley to the local paper. Down the steps, three planks out, a smudge broke the dust where a boot toe had turned. Not a tread I knew. I photographed it and the paint that had rubbed onto the bottom of the gate latch, a small smear of the house's green on something that came through too fast.

Back inside. I took the kitchen table chair and swung it an inch. A thin squeak the room knew answered me. I marked the sound in my head and moved on. We had an invite to find.

"Dining room," I said. We stepped in and saw a row of framed family photos on the buffet and a folded paper tent card near the runner. It was a printed invite for a book club hosted by Daria's venue. The logo sat in the corner beside a photo of a stack of old novels that had never met that room. The invite listed last night's date, gave an address, and used a phrase I know too well. VIP reveal. I took a photo flat, then one with a macro on the small print at the bottom where the host name and permit number live. Host, Daria Lin. Venue, her space. Permits, in order. I did not like that.

"Your aunt planned to bring a show and tell," I said.

"She told me she would listen more than talk," Talia said. "That was what she said when she meant she would let someone else make noise."

I took a wide shot of the dining room, the buffet, and the front window line so I could prove nothing had been shifted by us. Then I stepped back to the foyer and called Asa. When I call with that voice, he answers on the second ring.

"Tell me location," he said.

I gave him the address, the time, and the facts: keys on hook, car in drive, mug in kitchen, back door latch chipped, book club invite with Daria's name and last night's date. He did not ask why I was there. He knows I count before I feel.

"Stay put," he said. "Step outside. I will put a welfare alert on the channel and ask patrol to swing close. Do not touch another knob. Your cabinet copy stays locked."

"It stays locked," I said.

He hung up. Asa is many things. Efficient is one of them. I looked at Talia. "We step out now," I said. "We keep an eye on the front and a shoulder on our calm."

We stood on the porch again and watched a jogger dodge a stroller. The world does not stop for a missing person until a siren tells it to. I could feel the moment the alert hit the air. Two blocks down a patrol car eased off the main and took the cross street toward us. Not fast. Present.

"Do we think she went to the club," Talia said.

"I think she planned to walk in at seven," I said. "I think the invite tells a story. I think we do not write the final page yet."

Talia pressed her thumbnail into her palm and left a half moon. "She would not leave without telling me," she said. "Even when she wants quiet. She writes a note for the neighbor if she takes the cat to the vet."

"Neighbors," I said. "We knock."

The house to the right held a basketball hoop and a pair of scooters under a tarp. A woman with a baking tray opened the door on the third knock and blinked in the light. I gave my name and asked if she had seen Mara since last night.

"She left in the evening with a tote," the neighbor said. "Dress with flowers. She waved and said, club night, wish me luck. A car pulled up. Not a taxi. A hatchback with pins on the tote in the back window. I noticed the pins. Cats and a typewriter."

"Do you know the make or color," I asked.

"Silver," she said. "Not new. No spoiler. The driver wore a scarf in her hair and talked with her hands. She did not look at me."

"Time," I said.

"Between six forty and six fifty," she said. "I was setting a timer for the oven and remember scolding my son for smearing his fingers on the glass."

I thanked her and gave her my card. If a fact in a house has a second memory attached, it holds better. We crossed back and checked the left neighbor. He remembered a car door and laughter at seven fifteen. He did not see faces. He did not know where they went. He remembered the porch light going off at ten because his dog gets moody when lights change.

The patrol car stopped out front. Asa stepped out of the passenger seat though I had not seen him on the drive over. He must have been two blocks away when I called. He walks like a reader. He takes in a line and then the next. He looked at the porch, the mat, the living room window, and then at me.

"Walk me through," he said.

I did it in order and used my notes. Keys on hook. Mug with tag. Calendar note. Invite card with Daria's name and VIP reveal copy. Back latch chip. Green smear on gate latch. Boot turn in dust. Neighbor statement about a silver hatchback and a woman with a scarf, pins on a tote. Second neighbor with a time at seven fifteen and a porch light that went off at ten.

He wrote none of it down. He remembers in blocks. He will write later after the search. He looked at Talia when I spoke about the invite and watched her eyes. He sees truth that way. He nodded toward the patrol officer, who stepped inside with care and started the sweep with the call he has done a hundred times.

"Your cabinet copy stays where it is," Asa said.

"Locked," I said. "Tag reads pending. Colophon drift. Fore-edge shave with a flat on page thirteen."

"Good," he said. "We go to Daria's after this. She and I get along until we do not."

"Guest list," I said.

"Ask for it ready," he said. "If she hedges, I will ask the fire inspector to look at her occupancy record to loosen a tongue."

The officer came back after a quiet turn through rooms and shook his head. No one hiding. No cat under the bed. No second car in the garage. Asa thanked him and stepped inside himself to look once with his own eyes. He came back and squeezed the brim of his cap, an old habit he has not dropped even when caps do not travel with him.

"I am putting a welfare alert on the wires," he said. "We will ping cameras at traffic lights between here and Daria's place. We will ask the hospital hub to flag if Mara's name shows on intake. We will talk to the club host and the printer. We will talk to the picker and look at his phone again."

He looked at Talia. "You were wise to call," he said.

"She leaves notes," Talia said. "There was no note."

"That is often enough," he said. "You go with Liora for now. You will not sit here alone and wait for your mind to build a house with the floor missing."

She nodded. "I do better when my hands have a job," she said.

"Then you will help her write the list of everything in those boxes with a price we can live with later," he said. "Firm lines help people breathe."

We locked the house and left the spare under the frog after Asa took a photo to prove it. He pulled the front door to make sure the latch met clean and we stepped down together. The porch light clicked in the middle of the afternoon for no reason that I could see. I pressed the photo of the invite hard into my memory and tucked the macro shot into a sleeve in my notebook. I want the host name visible when I say it next.

We walked to the car. Peppermint had not joined us for this errand. I will not bring him to a house with a bad air. He knows when to stay, though he would claim another reason if he had words.

Talia buckled her belt and watched Asa return to the patrol car. "He does not waste words," she said.

"He knows words wear out on days like this," I said. "He saves them for when they count."

I took out my phone and tapped the photo I had taken of the invite. Daria Lin, host, with a time stamp that matched the neighbor's memory for oven timers. I enlarged the lower corner where the line about VIP reveal sat. That phrase means cameras, not books. I know her kind of event. She likes a spotlight bright enough to wash the ink off the page.

We drove back toward the shop in a silence that did more than noise would have done. When we reached the corner with the mural of the heron, I told Talia the plan in small sentences.

"Book stays under lock," I said. "Nothing from the boxes moves. We write the chain on a clipboard and tape it to the top. You make a list with me. Names to call. Times to log. I send the macro to the press foreman with a subject line that wins me an answer. Then we go smile at Daria in her room and ask for a guest list before her mouth catches up to her eyes."

"I can sit at the counter and make columns," she said. "I can keep my hands from looking for busy work."

"Good," I said.

"And if she is not there," Talia said. "If she left the club and did not come here and did not go to bed."

"We keep the alert active," I said. "We pull traffic frames. We talk to the hospital desk. We ask security at the club. We touch each knob once. We do not jump."

She huffed a small laugh at that. "You say that like you have jumped before," she said.

"I have," I said. "It looks bad on camera."

We parked in the back and came in through the stockroom. Rafi lifted his chin and read my face. He saw enough. He slid a clipboard across the counter before I asked and brought two pens that write without skipping. I opened the hold cabinet, made sure the tag faced out, and closed it again. It felt like setting a stone on a paper stack. Necessary and not enough and still right.

I wrote the headline on the clipboard. Estate boxes intake. Chain start at counter. Talia as consignor. Lot includes suspect first with pending tag. Do not move without me or Theo. I added the time and signed. Talia took the pen and wrote her name next to mine with a line that trembled for the first inch and then steadied. She leaned on the counter like a swimmer at the pool edge.

I forwarded the colophon macro to the foreman and added two lines of text. Confirm left bias low row for year. Confirm expected ink bite and rear stamp depth. No pleasantries. He likes a blunt ask.

I sent a shorter note to Asa. Invite photo attached. Host name and last night date. Door latch with paint chip. Smudge on gate. Boot turn in dust. Neighbor on hatchback with pins. He replied with a thumbs up and a short line. Welfare alert live. Patrol eyes on Daria.

I looked at the cabinet and felt the kind of tired that comes from thinking before noon. I put my hands on the counter and let the laminate hold one ounce of my weight. Peppermint surfaced from behind Romance and stood on his hind legs to scratch the corner of the stool. He looked up at me and blinked slow. He likes days that demand lists.

"Book stays locked," I said to the room and to the part of my brain that wants to grab and run.

I wrote it on a small card and pinned it to the cork behind the register. Locked means locked when the first tense person asks to see the pretty thing. Locked means I do not let charm talk me out of evidence. Locked means a person who opens cabinets without permission gets my hand on their wrist before they reach the shelf.

Talia watched me write it and smiled without humor. "You say it like an oath," she said.

"It is," I said.

The door bell rang and Miss Dotty stepped in again with a spare sweater and a tin that likely held something she would call soup and I would call mercy. She took one look at the two of us and set the tin near the receipt printer with no speech. She does not fill air. She makes room in it.

"Eat when the next call ends," she said. "People give smarter answers when you are not hollow."

I thanked her with my whole face. She patted my sleeve and then Talia's hand. The room steadied. The clipboard sat between us like a map. Asa's alert ran on a channel I could not hear but could feel. The invite photo sat on my phone where I would not forget host and hour.

We worked. I listed. Talia checked ISBNs against the back-of-the-brain list she had started to build in the last two days. Rafi kept customers happy without telling them about the missing person two blocks away. Peppermint took the stool and watched the cabinet as if his gaze had weight. The press foreman's email pinged at half past the hour with two words. Left lean. Then a third on its own line. Always.

I printed the email and taped it to the macro sleeve. I wrote the time and the sender and the words on my chain card. Press confirms left bias. Our copy drifts right. Ink reads smooth. The lock on the cabinet felt heavier and kinder.

The phone on the corner of the counter vibrated. Asa again. Short lines. Welfare alert in place. Patrol at Daria's venue. Host present. We would be smart next, not loud. I told Talia we would walk over after we wrote the last three items on the clipboard. She squared her shoulders and wrote the ninth title in a neat hand that had not shaken since she walked through her aunt's back door.

We left the book where it belonged. Under lock. With a red tag.

With a macro that carried proof. We carried our pens and the invite photo and the calm you can only fake for a minute. Today we would not have to fake it. We had a line to follow and a host to face. We stepped out into the street and let the bell on our door speak for us. One clean note.

CHAPTER 6

Printer Past

Walter Mott's garage sat behind a one-story house that could have been any house on our side of town if not for the hand-painted sign over the side door. Mott & Son, Letterpress, since a year that looked better on metal than on a tax form. The driveway held two oil spots, one faded, one fresh. A stack of bundled newsprint leaned under a tarp that flapped at one corner like a tired flag. I knocked on the side door with two knuckles. Inside, something heavy tapped twice and a chair scraped.

Walter opened with a rag over one shoulder and ink in the grooves of his fingers. He was the sort of man who looked like he had been born with a cigarette in his hand, though he was not holding one. He wore a shop apron that had seen more days than I have patience for, a faded ball cap with a printer's devil stitched above the brim, and a watch that should have retired when lead type did.

"You must be Wren," he said. "You smell like binding glue and cinnamon."

"You must be Mott," I said. "You smell like ink and vinegar."

He grinned at that, quick. Not friendly. Curious. He stepped aside and let us in. Talia followed a step behind me with her palms to her sides like she was trying to keep them from reaching for anything. Peppermint padded in without asking, tail high, whiskers forward. He likes rooms with many small things.

The shop was a rectangle of benches and shelves, each shadowed by its own lamp. An old Chandler sat against the far wall with a tarp draped over it like a coat on a patient who had not learned to mind his draft. A Vandercook proof press crouched under a dust cover, rollers wrapped and tied. Racks held galleys with lines of type asleep in their sticks. Above one bench, a pegboard carried tools that had been hung by a person who believed in both gravity and neatness. The air had a fishhook bite. Not rotten. Acid. Vinegar with a memory of something sharper.

Walter waved a hand toward a long drawer cabinet. "Plates. Cuts. Odds I never threw away," he said. He slid a drawer and revealed copper plates in waxed paper sleeves, each labeled in his block print. Birthday invite. Menu for Victor's. A logo with a dog that had lost its owner a decade ago. He ran his finger along the brass border of one plate like a person petting a good book.

"Nice to meet someone who kept his drawers in order," I said.

"Nice to meet someone who knows what the drawers hold," he said.

He opened a second drawer and showed donor sheets, a jumble of papers from jobs past. Offcuts and make-readies. Samples from mills that had closed or rebranded. He lifted one sheet and held it up to the light, squinting through a squall of flecks in the pulp. "When we ordered this, we thought we had landed in a better country," he said. "Then the mill sold and the new one sent us something that drank ink like water."

He slid the sheet back and closed the drawer. I watched his hands more than his face. Hands tell you when a person is lying to himself. These looked steady. They also looked ready to set something down and walk away from it, which is a different kind of lie.

"We came about a book," I said. "A first that fails a few tests. I do not bring you the book. I bring you a question. A dot grid. That press in that year, what did the colophon grid look like."

Walter did not pretend to consider. He gave the answer like he was reading from a poster on the wall I could not see. "Nine rows, seven columns, inner ring light, outer ring heavy, top left dot shy of a perfect corner. You could spot it from a foot away if your eye knew to look. If the foreman was sober. He never was."

He grinned again and the grin went old. "We argued about that shy corner for a month," he said. "I wanted it fixed. The owner said it gave us character. The owner won. Then he sold the press to a man with less character than the dot."

Talia leaned forward, the way people do when a detail reminds them that the world used to have fewer fonts and more men in aprons. "The inner ring light," she said. "Not even. Meant like that."

"Meant like that," Walter said.

"And if you saw a colophon with the inner ring heavy and the top right dot fat," I said, "you would say."

"I would say it came out of a shop that wanted to be ours and went right instead of left," he said. "Or a fool with a laser looked at a photo for two minutes and thought patterns are a game."

He shuffled a stack of sample cards without looking at them. I could hear them crackle. He knew the grid. He did not ask why. He did not ask which book or who brought it to me. That was a choice, not courtesy.

"Have you ever been asked to build a colophon sheet," I said. "Separate from a job."

"People ask for many things," he said. "People want to tie a ribbon around history and put it on their mantle. They want paper to confess that it sat in a room when it did not. They say anything can be done if you are not too proud to eat."

"Do you," I said.

He tapped the drawer with the donor sheets. Not hard. A rhythm, not a confession. "I have made letterheads for people who should not have had letterheads," he said. "I have pressed seals for clubs that should have stayed small. I have helped a man who could not see fix the cards for his wife's memorial so the commas would sit where she would have put them. I do not print counterfeit money. I do not sign names that belong to other men."

"Colophons," I said.

He shrugged once, fast. It could have been a gnat. It could have been regret.

I took the macro photo from my pocket, slid it into a clear sleeve, and set it on the bench under the nearest lamp. He did not reach for it. He looked at it. His eyes tracked the dots and the ink around them, the halo where pressure and paper kissed too evenly. He did not ask to touch the sleeve.

"That ring is wrong," he said.

"And the bite," I said.

"Wrong," he said. "That is toner or digital pigment or something else that never met a platen. Ink is a body. This is a shadow."

He leaned back. The rag on his shoulder slipped and fell on the bench. He did not pick it up. He looked at the pegboard for a beat and then at me.

"If I were a collector, I would stop at that photo," he said. "If I were a dealer, I would ask where you got it and what else lives in that box. If I were a policeman, I would ask who had access to donor sheets and who knows the grid."

"We are none of those in this room," I said.

"You are all of them," he said. "You only change hats."

He moved to a side bench with a wooden top worn smooth by a lifetime of pushes and pulls. He tapped a small tool that looked like a fountain pen had married a scalpel. The tip was dark and reminded me of a night in the bindery when a bottle of acid waked my nose from three rooms away.

"Acid nib," he said. "You know it."

"I do," I said. "You can age a cut or burn a margin line with it if you have patience and no love for your lungs."

He set the nib down and pushed it a hair away from the edge of the bench as if his fingers were afraid it might bite him. The move was practiced. I noted it.

"I use it for a trick we never charged for," he said. "People bring their father's diploma and ask me to touch the edge right where the binder made a mess in 1952. The acid lines the scar and takes the shine down. My wife used to call it a mercy pen. The word stuck and now when I pick it up all I can hear is that. Mercy."

Talia ran a finger along the top edge of a shelf and came away with clean skin. Walter's shop was not neat out of pride. It was neat because a stray curl of paper can sink a roller.

"You said vinegar," I said when we walked in. "I do not smell only vinegar. Something stronger sits under it."

He moved to a red toolbox and set his hand on the top drawer for a second before he opened it. He lifted a small bottle labeled with a skull and a hand, and a second bottle with a paper label and an old date. "Acetic," he said, and held up the second. "Cheap. Vinegar with pretensions. I use a dot on set screws sometimes, not to fake age. To move what should move and now refuses. If a man wanted to make rust where there was none, he would use the cheap one and a night."

He put them both down with care. The room stung a little more when the caps were off the first time. The cap was on now. The sting stayed. That meant recent use. I looked at the Chandler. Its screws looked clean. The Vandercook. Clean. The pegboard. Clean. The small tray beside the acid nib. A cotton swab lay on a piece of glass with a ring of brown at the walnut end.

Walter saw my eye on it and covered it with the rag he had dropped without any theater. He did not look embarrassed. He looked like a man who had just remembered he left a window open in a storm.

"Who asked you about the grid this month," I said.

"You did," he said, smiling in a way that wanted to annoy me.

"Before me," I said.

He folded his arms and looked up at the ceiling, which had a water stain shaped like a country no one would visit on purpose. "Men in hats," he said. "Boys with apps. A woman with a tote and a way of talking that made old fellows feel like they still had their fastball."

"Name," I said.

"People do not say their names when they see my drawers," he said. "They say I heard you were the man, and I say my son is the man and he lives in Ohio, and they say no, you, the one who can make the past sit still long enough to take a photo. That is what they want. They want a photo that behaves."

"What did she want," Talia said. "The woman with the tote."

Walter glanced at Talia like he had not noticed she was a person who could ask him a question. He gave her the same grin he gave me at the door. "She wanted a sample," he said. "She wanted to see what a real colophon looked like close. She had a phone and a light and the kind of attention that eats a room. I told her to buy a book and look at that. She said she had a book. I took pity on a fool."

"You showed her a sheet," I said.

"I took out a card from a job we did when I could still throw lead without my back talking to me," he said. "I said this is what a bite looks like. She nodded like the nod would add weight to the paper. She asked if I had donor paper from the right year. I told her donor paper had nothing to do with the year. She blinked. I said I had scraps that drank ink the way you want for a kiss. She asked me if I could make that kiss again."

"Did you," I said.

Walter held my eye for a count of three. Then he looked past me at the old proof press and the pegboard again. "I do not do Kinko's," he said. "I do not do Etsy. I do what I have always done, for people who know what they are asking for. And sometimes for people who never will."

"Which night was she here," I said.

He shrugged again, the gnat on his shoulder, the old regret. "You think I write everything down," he said. "My wife used to say I wrote nothing down that could hurt me later. She did the books. She died. The books got sloppy. The phone fills with numbers and lies."

"You know the grid," I said. "More than know. You talk about it like it is a friend you miss. Why shrug now."

He rubbed the heel of his hand across his eye and left a pale smudge of clean skin under ink. "Because I can tell you the name of the foreman who set that grid wrong fifty times and I can tell you the name of the kid who locked up the forme after the press ran hot and I can tell you what the coffee tasted like that week, but I cannot tell you what day the woman with the tote asked me to open a drawer so she could look at a photo and say first like it was a prayer. I am tired of people who use good words like they were keys."

I let that sit. He was not a man who would answer a second question better than the first. He would answer a third worse. He needed a step away.

Peppermint took that step for us. He had been circling the center table in a lazy figure eight, pretending to care about a screwdriver and a pencil. Now he hopped onto a shelf under the bench and sniffed a coil of twine as if he expected it to smell like tuna. He sneezed, a sharp sound that startled a curl of paper near the proof press. He sneezed again and hopped back, tail low, whiskers forward as if he had discovered the world was not kitten-proof.

Walter laughed and then covered his mouth like the sound had come from a stranger. "That cat has better sense than most men," he said.

"Twine smells like pickles," I said. "That means someone soaked it. People do that when they want to lay a line on paper and leave a stain that looks older than it is."

He did not answer. He walked to the shelf, lifted the coil, and brought it to me. The loose end was stiff and dark, the way cotton gets when you drag it through vinegar and let it dry in a hurry. He set it down and turned away from it like it had hurt his pride.

"Do you know this title," I said. "The one people say they found in a box that fell into their lap like a blessing. The one a niece brought me because she is young and decent and knows she should not sell a book she does not understand."

"I have heard many titles in this room," he said. "I have forgotten more. A blessing is a word for people who do not want to say theft."

"You know the grid," I said again, softer. "You know the ring. You know the way donor paper from the old mills drinks ink. You know an acid nib like a mercy. You know what a coil of twine looks like when it has been baptized in vinegar. You also know when a question is walking you toward a door you do not want to open."

He looked at me and there was something like pleasure in his eyes. I had spoken to him like he was not old. He liked that.

"You are not wrong," he said. "You will also not get what you want today."

"I am not here for a confession," I said. "I am here to write a list."

He nodded at that as if the sentence had passed an exam. He lifted the rag and wiped the bench in a slow circle. The vinegar pricked my throat again. He saw me notice and held out a bottle of hand cleaner, oil-based, scented like oranges.

"Take the bad out of your nose," he said. "People blame the smell for sins the eyes should carry."

I rubbed a dab into my palms and the citrus pushed the sting back a step. Peppermint climbed onto my shoulder with the confidence of a cat who thinks a shoulder is part of his home.

He bumped his head against my jaw and watched Walter with yellow eyes. The coil of twine sat on the bench like a line from a poem no one wanted to read out loud.

"We will come back," I said.

"You will," he said. "Bring the photo that shows the spine stamp, too. The one from a different day. The one that tells you the hands changed the story to match the mouth."

I did not ask how he knew about the spine. There are three possible answers. Seth showed him. Daria showed him. He saw it on a small screen that travels without asking for proof. All three answers fit. All three help later. I took a photo of the coil. I did not ask to take a photo of the nib. I had eyes. That was enough.

On the way out, Walter stopped at the door and set his palm flat on the jamb, a small habit that looked like a prayer he would deny if you named it. "I built a thing once for a boy in a band who wanted posters his father would not hate," he said. "I made the ink bite and the letters sing and the boy cried when he saw it because he had been told paper was the enemy. It is not the enemy. It is a mirror. People do not like what they see."

"I do," I said.

"Then you keep doing your job," he said.

We stepped into the light. The air tasted better. Talia exhaled with a sound like a zipper closing. Peppermint shook his paws as if the floor had left a film. I wrote the line on the small card I keep for chapter ends because it helps me keep the book inside the book.

Walter Mott knows the real grid by heart. He keeps an acid nib and vinegar twine on a bench. He shrugs when a truth touches his sleeve. He opened the drawers without fear and refused the question without lies. The room bit my nose. Peppermint sneezed.

CHAPTER 7

Margin Dates

The rare nook sits three steps up from the main floor, a small stage of oak and quiet. The glass case along the inside wall held three firsts that knew how to behave. Across from them the work table waited under a bright task lamp. I laid a clean blotter, then the book, then two evidence sleeves, then a card for notes. Gloves on. Phone set to camera. Peppermint leaped to the arm of the reading chair and arranged himself like a bookplate lion.

"Watch, do not help," I told him.

He blinked once. Agreement, or the cat version of it.

I opened the book on the blotter with the care that keeps me from losing sleep. The binding gave a soft sigh a few pages in, then settled. The colophon that had irked me still sat wrong. I left that for the folder marked press. Tonight was for the hand that wrote in the margins.

The first mark lived at page seven, a neat line under a sentence that people quote when they want to sound like they read past the first chapter. In the outer margin the writer had added, "I read this at Harbour & Hearth before the renovation, Earl Grey too strong, almond croissant a salvation." The pen line sat dark and smooth, no feather, no grit. The letters rounded clean at the joins, with small dots of pooled ink where the writer lifted and set down the tip. Ballpoints rarely pool that way. Gel does it without apology.

Harbour & Hearth did not exist when this book was supposed to have shipped. I did not need a search to know that. I stocked their first fundraising cookbook and kept a flyer from their opening month on the corkboard by the espresso machine. That month was ten years after this edition's claimed print date.

I snapped a photo of the margin with the café line in frame and slid a ruler along the gutter for scale. One shot under the task lamp, one with the flash, one with a small white card tucked under the text so the pen stroke showed clear. Peppermint's tail tapped the chair twice, then went still when I glared.

I turned the page slowly. One more note on eleven. "He is wrong about the fog. It comes in at three, not at dawn, ask anyone who works the ferry." That line meant a person who knows this coast. The pen said they wrote it with a tool sold long after the book left the press it claims. Both truths can live together when the name on the title page lies.

I checked the letterforms. The lowercase g hung with a loop shaped like a tear. The lowercase a had a single-storey form. Those lean modern, but that is slippery ground. Time stamps for ink are cleaner.

At the top edge of fifteen, a small dot sat where a pen had tested itself, as if the writer made sure the line would flow before marking the passage. I did not touch it. I pressed a strip of transparency film over the area and snapped a macro. You can see how gel sits up before it sinks in. You can also catch the slight sheen on older gel when the light hits at an angle. Ballpoint sinks into fiber fast and leaves a scratch you can feel. Gel skates. The stroke on that a carried no scratch under the gloss.

Miss Dotty chose that moment to float up the steps and stop two paces from the table. She dresses for libraries the way some people dress for church. Cardigan that has met a mending needle more than once, hair shaped into a tidy cloud, small chain for her glasses that looks like it belongs on a saint.

"I brought you the city pamphlets from the year you want," she said, holding up a slim folder. "Also the phone book. Also a loyalty punch from a café that thinks novelty is a spice."

"You had a feeling," I said.

"I follow our town on paper," she said. "You follow it with your nose. Between the two, we do not have to guess."

I pointed to the margin line at page seven. "Harbour & Hearth," I said.

She set the folder on the far corner, then leaned with both hands on the back of the chair so she did not get near the blotter. "Opened ten years after the date on that title page," she said without looking. "They took over the old tailor shop, kept the mirror, replaced the counter with a bar that cost double what they told the board. Three owners by now. Croissants better under the first."

"You keep the files and the grades," I said.

"I keep the civics," she said.

She stepped sideways and peered down at the ink. "No feather," she said. "No light cracks along the stroke. That shine is an insult. You want an old book to talk, you use an old hand. This is too smooth for the year on the colophon. You know that already."

"I do," I said. "I want it to land for a person who does not live in my head."

She lifted her chin with a small smile. "Find the launch year," she said. "Then you do not have to sermonize."

Rafi arrived with a tray for the case and a roll of evidence tape. He set both on the outer table and reached for the city pamphlet like a man who knows a folder can save an hour. "We kept the trade catalog from the year the gel pens changed, remember," he said. "Box under the register with the product cards. We made a display that lasted a week until a child tried to write on the window and we put the pens behind glass."

"Get the box," I said. "Bring me the card for the model that writes this line."

He left with a nod. Peppermint watched him go, then laid his face on the chair back and purred. He likes men who fetch boxes.

I turned more pages. The writer had discipline. They did not chatter at every paragraph. A thin underline here, a vertical bar there, a single word in the margin that told me what mattered to a person with a neat mind. Midway through the chapter a note about a street name argued with the author's memory. The writer corrected the direction and added, "The bakery moved across the alley in 2002, blame the landlord." That date walked up and shook my hand. The book claims to have shipped before that move went to council. The note claims to have known about it. The book and the note cannot both tell the truth on year.

I took a wide shot of the spread and wrote on my card. Café opened a decade after print. Bakery moved across alley in 2002, after print. Pen line smooth gel with pooled ends. Two modern tells in ten pages.

Rafi returned with a shallow box from under the counter. Inside lay a grid of product cards with dates and launch notes. I flipped until I hit the line we sell, then again until I found the model that runs smooth and wet in dark ink. The card had a photo of the refill and the packaging, a short list of line widths, and a small printed date that vendors include for their reps. Eight years after the run of this title.

I took a picture of the card beside my today's paper and slid both into a sleeve. "We will not claim brand," I said. "We will claim chemistry and date."

Miss Dotty fished a punch card from her folder and handed it to me with two fingers. Harbour & Hearth, first design. The card carried a grid of circles for stamps and a promise of a free pastry after ten visits. The small print at the bottom gave an opening month and a line about only one punch per visit that still cracks me up on dull days. I set the card beside the margin photo and took another shot. You do not need a web page if the café printed its truth in a font I can touch.

Miss Dotty tipped her head toward the pen box. "Your gel line changed packaging that year too," she said. "The little eye on the carton moved to the left."

"Of course you know that," I said.

"I know it because Rafi complained about shelf space and you told him we sell stations, not stickers," she said. "I was paying for a hardcover and listening in."

Peppermint shifted on the chair and thumped one paw against the cushion like a metronome. He does that when he wants us to admit that the line has landed.

I turned the book to the back and checked the endpapers. The hinge still held. Good. The last blank carried no ownership mark. No ex-libris sticker. That sits odd for a person who writes in a book like this. Wary people claim their margins and their boards. Secret people take their pen to someone else's copy. Once you say that sentence out loud, you have to deal with the kind of collector who brings a fake into a room and hopes the room likes being fooled.

I closed the book and let it rest open on its fore edge so the binding could breathe. Then I slid the gel pen product card back into the box and taped the sleeve I had shot shut with a neat strip. Rafi dated the tape and signed. He likes to be first in line for the chain when the thing on the table touched hands that might belong to a charge sheet.

"Do you want me to pull the vendor invoice for that pen's first arrival here," he asked. "We keep five years. Before that I can ask Felix at the stationers. He remembers his own kids' birthdays worse than he remembers launch months."

"Do both," I said. "We will bag the invoice. We will take a photo of Felix pointing at the old file if he smiles for the camera."

Miss Dotty's smile turned thin. "Do not put a man's face in a file unless you must," she said. "We will take the month and the card for now."

"Fair," I said. "We can get our ink age without a face. Later we will run a dye test on a copied dot. Tonight we only need the launch year to bracket the lie."

I logged what we had on a card in square lines. Margin mentions Harbour & Hearth, which opened a decade after claimed print date. Notes mention bakery move in 2002. Pen stroke reads gel. Pooled ends, no scratch. Line quality matches model launched eight years after this run. Photos taken with ruler and date card. Café punch card for first year shot beside margin photo. Product card shot beside margin photo. Both bagged.

Peppermint let out a sound that was half chirp, half meow. That is his version of an amen. He hopped down and landed light, then wandered to the stairs and sat there to take inventory of his kingdom. We had three customers in the front room, two reading corners filled, and Rafi's beans tapping the hopper like a heartbeat. The town had not stopped breathing, which counts for more than people admit.

My phone buzzed on the table. A notification swam up the screen and settled. Daria Lin had posted a photo of herself with the book. She had chosen a filter that made her skin look like pastry and the paper look younger than it is. The caption in cheerful lowercase read, "life-changer, read in the margins because that is where truth hides."

I stared at the image until the edges stopped quivering. She had framed the shot so that the colophon sat out of view. She had tilted the book so the deckle did not show. She had found a page with a line that makes undergraduates swoon and a note that made her sound like a person who sits among firsts as a natural right. The profile location tag placed her at her own venue, not here, which would matter later when we pulled times. Her smile asked a room to clap on cue.

Miss Dotty leaned in, read the caption, and let out a sound that

I will charitably call disapproval. "Margins are for conversation," she said. "Not for fraud."

Rafi saw the post over my shoulder and hissed through his teeth. "She tagged the store," he said. "Wants our light."

"We will give her a lampshade," I said. "Not the bulb."

I screenshotted the post with the timestamp and slid it into a new folder. Photo of Daria with the book. Caption that uses life-changer as if that word earns the paper. Location tag set to her place. Upload time rides the same hour as her brag on the club thread. I added a small card that said what I thought without the adjectives. She wants clout. She wants a stage. She will trade a woman's head for a headline if it turns a room.

Peppermint moved to the bottom step and stretched until his front paws touched the next riser. He sniffed the air, then sneezed twice in quick succession. That is his opinion of filters.

I closed the book on the blotter, set two clean bands around it, and slid it into the plastic cradle that fits our case. I have learned to box early when a page starts waving flags. A boxed book does not walk to a car. A boxed book does not let a hand write a second line beside a first. A boxed book waits for clean light and an officer's bag.

"You will show this to Asa," Miss Dotty said, more instruction than question.

"Yes," I said. "Tonight he gets copies. Tomorrow he gets the original if he signs the chain."

"Good," she said. "He was born to read case files, that one."

Rafi put the tray on the table so we could shift the book straight to the case without a dance. I put the cradle on the tray, breathed once, then moved it to the center shelf where two signed firsts made room. I locked the glass and tugged the handle twice. The latch kissed home with that small click that lets my shoulders drop a fraction.

On the table I left the punch card copy under weight so it would not curl, the product card copy bagged and labeled, and the note card with the list. I tucked the phone into the pocket of my apron and rolled my neck until the knot behind my left ear stopped sulking.

From the front, a customer laughed at something Rafi said that I could not hear. A school group passed along the sidewalk outside like ducks, all in step and impossible to count. A bus brake sighed at the corner. The book glowed under the case light like it wanted to be good. The margin lines glinted when the lamp swung and caught the gel.

"Life-changer," I said to the empty air. "We will see whose."

CHAPTER 8

Phone Spine

The book sat under glass where it behaved. The room had that steady quiet I like before noon. Rafi topped off the kettle. Peppermint took the windowsill and curled into punctuation.

I pulled my stool to the counter, opened my phone, and went to Seth's feed. People who live for rooms will always leave crumbs on their grids. There he was. Yesterday's post. Same title, same jacket, the bowl of oranges in the corner, and a hand near the gutter with a ring on the right. His caption fussed about a windfall that only a fast mover could land. The spine stamp in his shot sat lower and bit deeper than the one under my case light. Either he shot a different copy or someone swapped a piece. I had seen his metadata flash earlier across the top like an address label that refused to peel. It read yesterday, ten minutes before the time on Daria's invite.

I tapped the image. The platform had stripped the data, as always. Pretty picture, no truth. Time to ask for the file, not the post.

DM to Seth: Need the original, full file. For the chain.

A typing bubble. Then nothing. Then a sticker I did not need. Then a sentence with teeth filed flat.

Seth: Thought you had eyes, Wren. Why the homework.

Me: Because I do not bless ghosts. Send the file or I log your stall.

He sent a screenshot of his own post. Cute. I waited a beat so he could feel the weight of my silence.

Me: File, not a picture of a picture. Attach from your camera roll. Leave edits off. If your bite is true, the proof earns you credit when I write my note.

He enjoys a room that says his name. He enjoys it more when the room thinks he helped. Thirty seconds. Then a paperclip.

I saved the file to the case folder, named it with his initials, today's date, and the minute. I opened the info pane. There it was. Creation time that matched the invite math from my notebook. Ten minutes before the club. He had held a copy when he should have been getting his seat. The location tag had been toggled off. The file still hummed with the truth I needed. I wrote one line on the chain card in pencil. Marlowe original received via DM. Time stamp ten prior to club hour. Saved. Logged. Photo shows deeper bite, lower placement, cloth pull at joint.

I pinched the image to the edge of the spine. The stamp's number shape ran a hair different from ours. The bite read like a press kiss done by someone who knew the dance. The cloth pulled a whisper at the joint. The oranges glowed in the corner. The right-hand ring winked. Either he shot a second copy or someone rebuilt a spine for show. My stomach wrote a third option I did not like. A label swap.

Rafi set my tea on the mat without speaking. Peppermint flicked an ear. The bell at the door stayed still.

Me to Seth: Where is this copy now.

Seth: Handled.

Me: With whom.

Seth: Buyer. Don't worry.

Me: I worry on purpose.

Seth: You and your case light. The girl needs tuition, not sermons.

Me: She needs a clean sale. Tell me where it is or tell me you do not know.

He sent a shrug emoji. Then another line that wanted to be helpful without paying the bill.

Seth: If yours is weak, swap it out in the listing. Use my photo. I'll license.

Me: Not happening.

Seth: You will learn.

I did not write the sentence that crowded my mouth. I screenshotted the chat, saved the file, and printed the single page that mattered for the folder. I added the minute to the chain card and underlined DM file delivered. If this lands on a projector later, the line will pull its weight.

Miss Dotty drifted to the edge of the nook and tilted her head at my posture. "He behaved," she said, reading the set of my shoulders.

"He sent a real file," I said. "It said what we needed."

She did not ask what. She does not fish when the hook is already in the water. She nodded toward the case. "Then your note will stand when the chair does not match," she said.

"It will," I said.

We have another piece. Walter had asked for this shot in our file. Bring the spine stamp, he said. Hands change a story to match a mouth. I set the phone beside today's paper and took one more macro of the screen with the timestamp and the bite in frame. One picture that proves when as well as what.

Talia came up from the back with the roll of mylar and the way a person walks when they have taught their breath to march. "News," she said, careful.

"Proof," I said. "The photo he took was ten before the club."

Her eyes flicked to the case, then to my phone. "So either my aunt had two copies or someone touched ours."

"Those are the two I like least," I said. "There is a third I like even less. A part swap."

She closed her hand around the edge of the worktable and held for a count. "Then we find the part."

"We will," I said. "First we trap the hour so no one calls it a guess."

I pulled the invite photo from my notes and set it next to Seth's file info pane. The times lined up wrong in the exact way I wanted. The stamp in his file walked deeper and sat lower. Our case copy kept its shallow bite and high seat. The difference would fit on a ruler's thin edge, which is where good arguments live. I wrote the contrast on a card in my hand, then slid it into a sleeve and taped it shut. Rafi signed the tape. He likes first position on days that will end in a conference table.

I opened Seth's public post one more time. Comments flowed like fire ants. He had baited the room for likes. He had forgotten the part where a file never forgets its hour. I did not engage. I do not spar in feeds where the only tool is ego.

Me to Seth: One last thing. Do not delete that post.

Seth: Funny.

Me: Do not.

He sent another sticker, this time a handshake that looked like clip art left out in the rain.

I turned to the next job. The host.

The invite sat in my photos with her name crisp at the bottom. Daria Lin. The guardrails on this part are simple. Ask once with a soft voice. Ask twice with the law in the room.

Me to Daria: Send last night's guest list to my shop email now. Full names. Arrival times if you have them.

Three dots. Pause. A burst of glitter in a selfie I did not ask for. Then her reply.

Daria: Loved seeing you two last night. Big buzz. VIP reveal tonight is going to melt phones. Guest list is my secret sauce.

Press gets it at noon.

Me: I am not press. I am chain. Send the list.

Daria: Noon. Be a doll and tag the club. We got three new sponsors this morning.

Me: Noted.

I kept it dry. I took a clean card and wrote the red line Asa will want when I call him after lunch. Host insists on noon. Claims VIP reveal. Will press for occupancy record if she stalls. He had already set the plan for that part. Ask for guest list ready. If she hedges, the fire inspector looks at her numbers.

Peppermint stepped off the windowsill and thumped a paw against the case glass once. Agreement. Or hunger. Or both.

I sent one more ping to Daria with my shop email typed out in full. She hearted it, then added a line with three golden crown emojis.

Daria: VIPs, babe. Wait till you see who.

CHAPTER 9

Book Club Brag

Daria's venue sits behind a brass door that resists fingerprints and common sense. The sign reads The Bindery in serif gold. Today the doorman in oxblood shoes guards a stack of glossy postcards that shout about a "Firsts Night." He waves me in because he knows my face and my habit of writing things that hold up when lawyers breathe on them.

Inside, the room smells like old leather and citrus cleaner. Velvet banquettes ring the space. A long bar holds a line of coupes that sweat under orange peels. The ceiling fixture looks like a wheel from a printing press. No one here prints. They sponsor. They post. They buy stories about themselves and call it culture.

Daria Lin stands on a low platform with a paperback in one hand and a crystal flute in the other. She wears a white jacket that glows against the navy wall. Her hair is perfect. Her smile could sell expensive water. She is not reading the paperback. She is auditioning for it.

"Friends," she says, and her voice reaches to the corners and comes back with confetti stuck to it. "Last night set a new high for our club. We brought a true first into the light. A first does not bow. A first commands. You felt it when the case rolled in."

There is a cheer at "first." Her crowd loves a ladder word.

I take a seat near the back by a pillar. From here I can see the platform and the bar, and the hallway that leads to the private lot. Rafi would call this a corner for feral cats. Peppermint would approve.

Daria flips open the paperback and reads a line in a tone that belongs to a pulpit.

"'Begin at the beginning,' the margin says. 'If there were an easier start, ink would have found it.'"

She closes the book as if it bit her. The audience laughs as if the line came from a divine source, not a gel pen in the last five years. She has quoted the marginalia near the title page, the note I circled on day one because the hand tucks an odd loop into a lowercase g. The loop belongs to someone who signs with theater flair. The loop does not belong to the supposed annotator, long dead. The loop belongs to someone who likes stages.

"Scripture," she says, and touches the book to her chest. "We host work that carries breath on the page."

I write one word in my pocket notebook. Gel. Then I add a dot over the g like a tiny crown to remind me of her habit. It keeps my hands busy while I watch her talk.

She rides the word first like a prize horse for another five minutes. Every turn of her story lands on it. First donor. First to see. First to sign. First to call a thing by its proper name. I count nine firsts, then stop because my pencil would snap.

The crowd is a mix of money and hope. A publicist in pink holds her phone high to catch the light. A pair of men in linen sit hip-to-hip with hands that twitch toward each other when Daria lands a line. A woman in a camel blazer watches without blinking and drinks club soda like medicine.

I stand when the volunteers begin to pass trays. People left bank cards on file here. Trays move better when a bill waits under the system. I do not take the canapés. I am here to move Daria from noise to risk, not to feed her algorithm.

She spots me when I cut along the bar. Her smile widens. She does not wave. She tilts her chin. The room reads that tilt and parts for me.

"Liora," she says. "Our brightest bookshop light."

She holds out her hand like a monarch. I shake it like a clerk. Her skin is warm. Her thumbnail wears a clear coat with a line of gold at the moon. The skin at the side of her right thumb shows a thin nick, a healed slice that runs across the pad at an angle. A fresh peel sits beside it like a ragged comet. It is the kind of mark a short blade leaves when it glances off tape and into flesh.

"You missed the first toast," she says.

"I prefer my bubbles in court," I say. I let my eyes drop to the nick and then back to her face. "Busy morning?"

She follows my glance without flinching. "Boxes," she says. "Sponsorship is made of boxes."

"Yours or the club's."

"Ours," she says. "I brought a surprise for tonight. The room will faint."

I nod without giving her the oxygen she wants. "Guest list," I say. "Email. Now."

Daria's smile does not falter. She angles her body so the crowd sees us in profile. She wants people to snap us together.

"Noon," she says. "I feed the room before I feed the file."

"You feed both," I say. "If you stall, Asa calls the fire inspector and they count heads. It will ruin your reveal."

She thinks about whether that threat is theater or law. She knows Asa. She knows he would walk in with a clipboard and an even tone. She also knows her capacity number sits on a certificate at the entrance in a frame that looks expensive.

"Always with the rules," she says, still sweet. "Relax. We are on the same side."

"We will find out," I say.

She leans forward. "I handled the book," she says, lower now, for me, not the room. "We took good care. Gloves. Temperature. Gentle hands. The way you like."

I let the words hang. She wants me to ask how. She wants the title. Daria never learned that empty air is a more efficient tool than any question.

She fills it. "It came in with the donor. We did a private pass-through behind the curtain to avoid the clamor. My team rolled the case to the back. I held it at the cradle myself."

"You held the book," I say. I keep my voice level. "Bare hands or nitrile."

"Nitrile," she says. "Please. I am not a monster."

"Name of the donor."

She laughs. "We don't give up donors. You know that."

"I write for buyers and heirs," I say. "You know that too." I tilt my head toward the hallway to the lot. "Back there. The pass-through."

She nods. "Door by the storeroom. Cameras on all points."

"Then your file will be easy."

She tips her glass and watches the men in linen laugh at something her bartender says. The men glance back at her to see if they laughed correctly. She keeps her eyes on them while she speaks to me.

"You saw the margin line I quoted," she says. "It read like a letter to me. Like the writer was in the room. I cried. It felt like permission."

"Permission for what."

"To step into the story," she says. "To own a piece of its first hour in public."

"You like owning first hours."

"Who would not," she says. "A first is a crown."

She shows her right hand as if by accident. The nick glints. The peel catches. I watch the angle. Right-hand thumb. Blade moved down and away from the finger when it slipped. That movement belongs to someone who pulled a boxcutter toward her on a right-hand cut instead of slicing away from the body. Untrained. Or rushed. Or both.

"What did you cut," I ask. "The night of the club."

She smiles. "Boxes," she says again. "We unboxed cases, risers, and those fussy rope stanchions you hate."

"Who else cut," I ask.

"Staff," she says. "You know most of them. Kiki at the door. Yannis at the coat check. Paolo on photos. Marta on press."

"Paolo is a photographer," I say. "He would not be cutting stanchions."

"Then Kiki," she says, bored now. "You can ask them."

"I will," I say.

A server stops with a tray of thin slices of pear on blue cheese. Daria plucks one and holds it at a distance so the crowd sees she takes what she sells. She does not eat it.

"What did you think of the marginalia," she asks me, bright again. The stage voice returns and, with it, the audience.

"Modern gel ink," I say. "Different pressure on upstrokes. Wrong for the era. The words are anachronistic in the way most forgeries are. A little too tidy. A little too perfect."

The room stills by one degree. She has given them a story where the book is a miracle. I have offered a story where the miracle wears a party wig.

"You are a buzzkill," she says, light as a skipping stone. "Our guests had an experience."

"Experience does not outrank evidence," I say.

"Evidence can be bought," she says without the smile. "You of all people know how taste is built."

She thinks this will pin me. She thinks I will defend my trade. I give her nothing. I look at the stage curtain in the back, then at the hallway again, then at the hand she still has not eaten.

"I need the guest list," I say. "And the names of the people who touched the case."

"Touched," she repeats, savoring the word. "I touched it. Yannis rolled it. Kiki cleared the path. Seth hovered like a moth at a porch light. Paolo filmed my hands. The donor stood too close and pretended not to."

I let that land. "Seth hovered," I say. "At what time."

"Before the clock," she says. "He thinks his presence blesses a room. He should try an RSVP once in his life and save us all time."

"You think he arrived before posted time."

"I saw him in the hall," she says. She points vaguely at the route behind the platform. "Phone in his face, talking to his own reflection. He does that."

"Who unlocked the storeroom."

"I did," she says, with pride now. "I keep the keys. I arrange deliveries and reveals. It makes the work sing. It is a first in its own way."

"Then you will send me the key logs."

She laughs. "Key logs," she says, as if I asked for the moon. "You are adorable."

"Adorable is for kittens," I say. "Send the logs."

She lets the silence sit so her friends can watch her not be bullied. Her friends look at me like I tracked mud on the carpet. I wait.

"Fine," she says at last. "After the reveal."

"Before," I say. "By noon."

"Always noon with you," she says. "Fine."

I pull my phone and type an email subject line in front of her. "Key logs. Guest list. Staff on shift. Camera points and retention policy."

"You are a machine," she says. "How do you sleep."

"With the cat on my ankle," I say.

That gets a real laugh from two people at the bar. Pets humanize a boundary. I let them have it.

A hand tugs my sleeve. The woman in the camel blazer stands at my elbow. Close now, I see a streak of ash in her hair like a lightning scar. She holds herself like someone who reads before breakfast.

"Ms. Wren," she says. "I love your shop. I teach down the block on afternoons. Exit pedagogy in the morning. Entry to joy at lunch. Rinse and repeat."

"Thank you," I say. "Name."

"Professor Isla Penry," she says, and Daria's head swivels a fraction. "Media studies. I consult for the club on captions. Daria is a delight."

"Is she," I say.

Isla smiles at that and looks back at Daria, who is now ignoring us in the way a person ignores a smoke alarm they cannot reach.

"I heard your note on the margins," Isla says. "I thought the same and put a pin in it to search ink types later. Today I remain a guest." She lowers her voice. "Seth said first in his post and then first again in my ear. He is stuck on the word in a way that feels like bait."

"He likes bait," I say. "He showed up before posted time."

"He did," she says. "He blocked the hallway with a story about provenance that took the long way. I watched him step backward as Daria rolled the case past. He would not yield the center of the frame."

"Did he touch the case."

"He hovered," she says carefully. "He has hands that ask for trouble."

"Did Daria stay near him."

"For a minute," Isla says. "Then she broke off. Someone waved her to the lot. She went through the service hall with a man I did not know. A seller, from the way he held his bag and the way he did not make eye contact."

"A seller," I say. "What time."

"Five-thirty ish," she says. "Half-stride past a half hour. I checked my phone for a car share and saw the time. I am a clock watcher on days with gas leaks and children in strollers."

"Describe him."

"Tall, jacket too tight across the back, hair that wants to curl but got scolded by gel," she says. "A knuckle with a scrape. He wore a canvas tote with a university logo that did not match his shoes."

"You saw them go where."

"Through the service door to the lot," she says. "Not the main doors. The one by the storeroom. Paolo called it the 'back lot swing' when he told Kiki to hold the coat check a minute."

"Paolo saw it too."

"He did," she says. "He clocked everything. He always does, then he pretends he does not. It helps with tips."

I write faster now. Service hall. Lot. Seller with tote. Paolo. Kiki. Five-thirty plus.

"Thank you," I say.

Isla dips her head. "I suppose the word first does not mean clean," she says.

"It never means clean," I say. "It means early. Early is messy."

She laughs. "Put that on your window," she says. "My students can read it on their way to bad choices."

I look back to Daria. She is fielding applause for a line about rescue, the kind rich people use to frame a London purchase as a noble act. As the clapping dies, she lifts the paperback again.

"Listen," she says, and quotes another margin. "'A first printing is a hand on your back that says go.'"

She closes the book. She holds her thumb against the cover and I watch the peel catch and then release. If a blade slid on stanchion tape, it slid today, not last night. The heel of the cut looks fresh. The edge blushes where the skin lifts. She has handled a cutter since breakfast.

A staffer in black slips to her side with a tablet. Daria nods without reading. The staffer retreats.

I drift to the service hall and stand a foot back from the threshold. A small sign reads Staff Only. Another reads No Storage In Hall. A glance into the space shows a steel door with a code pad, a plain door with a keyhole scarred by clumsy hands, and a taped map that outlines an emergency route. The taped map bears a coffee ring like a halo. I take a photo from the permitted line. I do not cross.

"Can I help," a voice says at my shoulder.

Kiki from the door smiles with her whole face. She wears a pin that says Ask Me. Her braid is tight and practical. Her shoes are flat and clean.

"I will not block your hall," I say. "I need the names of those who used this door on the clock last night."

"On the clock is all of them," she says. "We were at capacity. People need air. Bartenders used the lot. So did smokers. Daria did a walk. Yannis rolled a cart out and back."

"With whom."

"Seller guy," she says. "Blue tote, thin elbows. She told me to hold the front for five while she took a call."

"Did Seth go out there."

"He tried," she says. "I had to keep him on the velvet side. He thinks velvet ropes are for everyone else."

"You saw Daria with the seller."

"Yep," Kiki says. "She had that face like she does when a sponsor wanders in. Sweet and sharp. He had a look like a person who lost a ticket. Helpful and hunted at the same time."

"Time."

"Five-thirty to five-thirty three," she says. "I watch clocks. Daria likes changes on the half. She calls them beats. We run on beats. We do not miss."

"Did Paolo see them."

"He sees everything," Kiki says. "He filmed the pass-through, then walked the lot to grab a light battery. He told me to hold a coat because the ticket fell off."

"Whose coat."

"Seth's," she says, with a grin she does not hide. "He hates tags. He wears his attitude like one."

"Thank you," I say.

I step back into the main room and text Asa with what I have. He responds with the word Copy and a time for a call. Noon. He keeps his beats like a surgeon.

At the bar, Paolo leans on his elbows with one hip balanced in that stance that looks casual and hides a lot of work. He has a strap line on his shoulder where a bag sat for too long. I slide to a stool at the end.

"Battery," I say.

He looks at me, then past me, then back. He decides to behave. "Light died on the lot and did not want to," he says. "I told the light to be polite. It refused. I fetched the spare. Kiki has a good memory."

"She said you filmed Daria's hands on the case," I say.

"I did," he says. "Hands matter. Sponsors pay for hands."

"And the seller."

"Which one," he says.

"The one at five-thirty," I say. "Blue tote. Thin elbows."

"Right," he says. "Jacket too tight. Hair scolded by gel. He walked like his shoes belonged to someone else. Daria walked him to the lot, then to the lower corner where the cameras miss. She calls it the shade. Sponsors who cheat call it the ashtray."

"Why does the camera miss it."

"Old unit, blind spot," he says. "The contractor said they would fix it. They did not."

"You filmed her hands. Did you film the lot."

"I filmed what I am paid to film," he says, and lifts his water. "And what tips ask for."

"Did you see what left in his tote."

"Nothing on the way out," he says. "Something on the way back."

"What."

"Paper," he says. "Flat. Size of a donor sheet. Brown around the edge, like it kissed acid in a drawer."

"How many sheets."

"One," he says. "He folded it in half and slid it into the tote behind the logo. Daria looked at the door and not at his hands. She can count seats and dollars at the same time. Hands are a third track. She stays on the first two."

"Did she keep anything."

"She held a slip in her palm when she came back," he says. "White, thick, board weight. The size of a claim check."

"For the lot."

"For a box."

We both watch her for a while. Daria rides the word first again, this time with a story about a patron who bought the club's first set of chairs and got naming rights on the fixtures. The patron beams in row three, and the room applauds like a cathedral.

"You will send me the clip of her hands," I say.

"With what credit," he says.

"None," I say. "Chain only."

He weighs that, shrugs, and nods. "I will send the clip," he says. "Because you pay in clean endings, and I like those even when my boss does not."

"Your boss likes confetti," I say.

"She likes being near it," he says. "Different addiction."

Daria calls for a round of toasts, then waves a server toward the private room. The low platform empties as people angle for the better view.

I slide to the hallway again and stop at the line. The storeroom door bears a fresh nick at lock height, a half-moon cut in the paint where metal met metal. The key plate shows a bright scratch. Someone missed on a fast insert. I take a photo. I do not touch the plate. I angle the shot to pick up the door edge and the tape on the floor that marks a safe path. The tape is new along one stretch and old along another. Someone patched. Someone rushed.

"Find what you need," Isla says, back at my elbow. She reads rooms like I do.

"Pieces," I say.

"Pieces make a picture if the edges hold," she says. "I like puzzles with corners."

"So do I," I say.

"Daria thinks corners spoil a vibe," Isla says. "Circles are kinder to donors."

"Circles hide exits," I say.

She smiles and leaves me to my work. I take a last note on the thumb nick, then write one line that matters in hard pencil so it will copy onto the card below. Right-hand thumb cut, fresh peel. Boxcutter in play today. Claim box. Key plate scratch bright. Lot blind spot. Seller with tote. Daria at five-thirty.

When the trays return to the floor and the crowd settles, I move toward the exit to catch the air that hangs in the corridor outside the main doors. The doorman raises an eyebrow at me, then at my lack of canapé. I raise one back at his shoes. He smiles. We reach a truce.

On the street a breeze pulls orange peel from the door frame and sends it skittering to the curb. A woman in a sunflower dress lights a cigarette and then remembers she quit and crushes it out in the tray. She looks at me like I have opinions about lungs. I do. I do not share them.

"Ms. Wren," someone calls.

The man in the camel ballcap from last night jogs up, a ticket lanyard swinging against his chest. He was near the bar when the case rolled in. He had the wide eyes of a person who wants to be first into every room and never is. Today he is out of breath.

"You do the words," he says. "I saw your posts. Loved the one about the brass corners on the travel trunk. The before and after."

"Thank you," I say. "Did you need the restroom."

He laughs and then tries to catch where I placed the joke. He finds it and does not repeat it.

"I saw something last night," he says. "I was late. I ran the long way and took the lot. I saw the seller leave with Daria toward the back. He had the tote. Blue. University logo. She had her phone like she was texting, but she was not. They turned toward the far corner where the trash bins sit. Camera there never works. My cousin used to clean. He said the camera needs a part. The part never arrives."

"What time," I say.

"Half past," he says. "I remember because I thought I could still make the first toast if I cut the coat check."

"What did he look like."

"Thin elbows," he says, matching Isla's words by accident. "Jacket too tight. Hair scolded by gel. He kept his head down. She kept her chin up like the queen of a prom."

"Did he come back."

"Later," he says. "He looked lighter. His tote did not sag as much. He had a paper in there when he went out. He did not when he came back."

"Thank you," I say.

He shuffles, pleased. "Do you think I can get into the private room if I say I saw it," he says.

"You will get into the private room when you buy a private room," I say. "Drink water. Thank you for your eyes."

He salutes with his lanyard and drifts toward the velvet rope. The doorman does his job. The man shrugs and takes a photo of the sign and moves on.

I text Asa. Seller seen leaving with Daria toward lot. Five-thirty. Blind spot. Paper in tote. Paper out. Thumb cut on Daria right hand fresh today. She claims box.

Copy, Asa replies. Hold your line. Noon call.

I look back at the platform. Daria holds court again, chin high, thumb curved against the paperback, the nick bright, the peel pale, the hand steady. She quotes another line from the margin and closes her eyes on it like prayer.

She clings to the word first as if the word can cover sharp edges. It cannot. It draws light to them.

Inside my pocket notebook, the card for this chapter of the day carries a new hook for the next. Ping Daria again for the list. Pull Paolo's clip. If she drags, we press the capacity number and count heads with the city at noon.

And now that I have three eyes on the lot, I can start to price her risk instead of her noise.

CHAPTER 10

Ink Age

The back office smells like clean paper and tea leaves. Rafi leaves the door half open so Peppermint can patrol and still keep an eye on the corridor. Miss Dotty takes her post at the small table with the ledger. She never hovers. She witnesses.

I clear the mat, set the tray, and lay out a strip of chromatography paper, a glass jar with a lid, a tiny pipette, distilled water, and the solvent set we keep for days when truth likes to smear. No theatrics. No glitter. A fan hums in the window. A metal rack waits beside the paper like a pair of steady hands.

"He wants noon," Miss Dotty says, meaning Asa.

"He will get noon," I say. "Before that, we lock this down."

I pull a sleeve from the safe. Inside sits the interleave I used when I copied the margin for my notes. High rag, smooth finish, thin enough to catch an offset if fresh ink kisses it wrong. It did. A single pinhead dot sat in the corner where my overlay met the lower loop of a g. I circled the dot yesterday and sealed the sheet. Today I cut a square around it, two millimeters on a side, clean edges, fresh blade, no drag.

"Photo first," Miss Dotty says.

I lay the interleave square on a white card, slide today's paper into frame, and take a shot from overhead. Ten October stares back from the masthead. I write the card ID in pencil, mark the time from the clock on the wall, and initial the corner. Rafi countersigns. Peppermint thumps her tail once against a box of mailers and pretends she did nothing.

"Open light or UV first," Rafi asks.

"UV," I say. "Let's see if it sings."

He dims the overhead. I switch on the longwave lamp and bring it close. The dot wakes. Not iron gall brown. Not old carbon. A soft coral blink rides the edge, the same trick new gel inks like to play so phones adore them under club lights. A tracer. A dye with an ego.

"Modern," Miss Dotty says, even, like a nurse reading a pulse.

"Modern," I agree. "We still run it."

I click the lamp off, bring the lights back up, and set the strip. Long edge cut straight, narrow enough to line up bands, thick enough to hold shape. The jar holds a mix I know by heart. Butanol, acetic, water. Upper layer, clear as gin. A chalk line sits across the strip near the bottom, drawn lightly with a 2H pencil so the solvent front can pass. I wet the pipette with distilled water and touch the dot once to wake the binders. A kiss, not a wash. The coral blush brightens and then settles.

"Loading now," I say.

I transfer a whisper of that bloom to the strip, a single touch on the base line. A second touch beside it. Two starts. One for my eyes. One for the file.

"Solvent ready," Rafi says.

We lower the strip into the jar with the care a person gives when holding a tired bird. The base line sits above the pool. The solvent front will climb by capillary and coax the dyes to walk. The lid seals. The fan keeps the room honest.

"Timer for eight," Miss Dotty says. She sets it, flips her ledger, and writes one line. Placement to jar, 10:14, ID card match, two-start load.

I send Asa a text that reads Incoming test, ink age, interleave offset dot run, UV coral blink, TLC climbing, stand by. He responds with a dot and the word Copy. He likes one-word answers. He saves syllables for closing arguments.

The climb begins slow, then steady. The front rides clean, no waver, no too-quick leap. I tap the jar twice to settle bubbles. Rafi looks at the clock like a line cook.

"Stop at two centimeters," I say. "I want separation without a mess."

At minute six the front hits where I want. I lift the strip with tweezers and set it in the rack, and mark the front line with pencil before the solvent breathes away. A faint blue-green band moves midway. A stubborn red flirts with the base. A violet haze rises toward the top.

"Gel cocktail," I say.

"Not nineteenth century," Miss Dotty says.

"Not close," I say.

I take the second strip from the jar, mark the front, and lay it flat on a clean tile. No fanning. No heat. Let it dry honest. Peppermint reaches a paw toward the tile, then decides against earning my look.

I switch the lamp back on. The coral tracer glows along the red band. The blue-green throws a shy light. The violet haze hangs like a ghost.

"Can you name them," Rafi asks.

"I can name families," I say. "Rhodamine for the coral. Phthalo mix for the blue-green. A violet from a brightener blend."

"Historic," Miss Dotty says, a question shaped like a word.

"No," I say. "Rhodamines sit on gel pens after the millennium. Trade catalog drops the first cross-market rush around aught-three. Brighteners in these blends show up in retail pens after that. Phthalo lives in old inks, yes, but blended like this it rides a different binder. Not iron gall. This rides a gel network."

"Modern to the bone," Rafi says.

"Modern to the bone," I repeat.

He brings the phone again. I frame the strip beside today's paper, then take one with the lamp on so the band glow reads. Two shots, full frame, no filters. I write the strip ID on the margin of each printout as they roll from our little printer.

"Bag it," Miss Dotty says.

I slide the dried strip into a coin envelope, add the card with the masthead photo, a print of the UV frame, and a clean copy of the chain line. I sign the flap across the seam. Miss Dotty signs under mine. Rafi tapes the flap and stamps our shop mark in red.

"Second strip," I say. "This one runs to Asa."

He nods. "Courier or walk."

"Walk," I say. "But only after noon. If Daria plays games with the list, I want all eyes on her before anyone leaves this building."

"Two prints for the case board," Miss Dotty says. "One under glass."

I clip the photo of the strip to the board above the evidence tray. The UV shot goes under the case light. I add a typed card with three simple lines. Coral tracer present. Gel binder behavior. Post-print era formula.

"Write it in pen," Miss Dotty says.

I take the fountain from the holder and write those lines again by hand. The court trusts ink. Jurors like ink. We built our house on ink that tells the truth about itself.

"Control test," Rafi says. He pulls a gel pen from the drawer and writes a dot on a spare strip. Same solvent. Same climb. Same bands glow, not a perfect match, but a sibling. He labels it house control. We bag that too and mark it control only, not evidence.

"Call him," Miss Dotty says.

I hit Asa's number. He picks up on the second ring.

"Tell me," he says.

"Interleave dot glows under 365," I say. "Rhodamine tracer, gel behavior. TLC shows coral near base, blue-green mid, violet haze up high. Not iron gall. Not period."

"Photos with date," he says.

"Yes," I say. "Two frames. Masthead in shot. Second frame under UV."

"Bagged and signed," he says.

"Yes," I say. "Two strips. One stored. One for you."

"Reach," he says.

"Post-millennium retail gel era," I say. "Not nineteenth century. Margins are a modern hand."

He pauses for a breath that tells me he is writing even if I cannot hear the pen. "Chain ID."

I read the numbers. He repeats them back. I hear keys, then a folder snap.

"Add language for a lay read," he says.

"Fluorescent dye used in current gel pens," I say. "Confirmed by simple lamp. Fix carries in bands. Paper strip test proves a modern formula that did not exist when the book was printed."

"Good," he says. "Send the images now. Courier strip after noon."

"Done," I say. "One more thing. Daria's thumb shows a fresh boxcutter peel. Right hand. She claims boxes."

"She packed something," he says. "Or repacked."

"She held court," I say. "She quoted margins like scripture and clung to first as if first forgives all sins."

"First forgives invoices," he says. "Send the thumb photo if you have one."

"I do," I say. "Cropped. No drama."

"Send it," he says. "We will log body condition under observational."

"Copy," I say.

"Guest list," he says.

"She promised noon," I say. "We press if she slips."

"I will ring the inspector at eleven fifty-nine," he says. "They like me. I never waste their shoes."

We end. I drop the photos into his secure share, then print one more set for our own safe binder. Rafi stamps the backs. Miss Dotty notes the time of transfer and the names of the files. Peppermint curls on the warm printer cover and purrs like a sleep engine.

"Want coffee," Rafi asks.

"Tea," I say. "Black."

He sets the kettle for a second boil and lines up two cups. My hands like work while the kettle thinks. I clean the jar, label the wash bottle with the date, and wipe the mat. No solvent stains. No stray fibers. We leave rooms cleaner than we find them because habit eats mistakes for breakfast.

He sets the mug beside me. I take the heat into my fingers and let my shoulders drop. The strip glows under the case light like a small neon sign. No mystique. No fuzzy story. A band here, a band there, fixed by the hand of capillary action and a recipe you can measure.

Miss Dotty closes the ledger and pats the cover. "Seal the margin as modern," she says, reading our scene goal without reading my outline. "Now speak like a human."

I sit. I speak into the small recorder we use for day summaries. "Margin ink is modern. UV tracer present. Gel network behavior confirmed by strip climb. Formula did not exist at print date. Photographed with today's paper. Strip bagged and sealed. Control run parallels behavior. Miss Dotty and Rafi witnessed. Peppermint unhelpful but handsome."

Peppermint opens one eye, offended, then sleeps harder.

"Send Talia a single line," Miss Dotty says. "Plain words. No adjectives."

I text Talia: Margin ink modern. We can prove it. No period harm. Taking care.

Her reply lands a minute later: Thank you. Do not let them spin it.

"Spin runs out of road when people ask for dates," I say.

The door chime in the shop gives two polite notes. The world wants paperbacks. The world wants cool air. The world wants the right scone. Rafi heads for the front. Miss Dotty stays on her stool like a carved figurehead, kind eyes and iron spine.

I pull the case light closer and put Seth's file photo on the stand next to the strip. His shot of the spine looks smug now. Deeper bite, lower stamp, oranges in the corner, ring on the right hand. The file tells me he took it ten before posted time. The strip tells me a hand with a pen added modern words to old paper. The two together tell me his word first is a sales pitch with glue on it.

I draft a short memo for Asa's folder. No flourish. Bullet truth.

- Interleave dot under UV shows modern tracer behavior.
- TLC separation on cellulose strip yields bands consistent with gel dyes in current pens.
- Date on masthead in photo: 10 October.
- Chain numbers on bag match L. Wren log.
- Control run with retail gel shows similar behavior.
- Conclusion for lay reader: margins written in current era, not at time of printing.

I drop the memo into his share and hit send.

Three minutes later my phone buzzes.

Asa: Ink info added to file. Margin flagged modern. Nice work.

I stare at that line and let out a breath I did not know I was holding. Not relief. Alignment. Evidence makes a spine inside a case. Once the spine clicks, the rest of the argument stands up.

The cat hops down and rubs against my shin to claim credit. I scratch his head once, then go back to the board. I move the ink card into the center and slide Seth's file photo beside it. I draw a line from Daria's thumb photo to the strip and mark it with a tiny blade icon. I add the word Lot and circle it where three statements touch. Paolo. Isla. Camel cap. Three eyes, one route.

Rafi leans back in. "Front's steady," he says. "We have ten minutes till noon."

"Good," I say. "Call Kiki and ask for camera retention policy text. Not the marketing copy. The line they send to cops."

He grins. "On it."

I read the clock again. We built our day around beats. Noon sits now like a coin on a drumhead, ready to leap if someone taps wrong. The room is calm. The strip is dry. The file is heavier by one clean page. Daria can brag until her voice cracks. Her margin sings under a lamp in a way no old ink sings.

Peppermint jumps back to the windowsill and stares at a pigeon as if it owes him rent. Miss Dotty flips the ledger to a fresh page and waits for my next sentence.

Noon will bring a guest list or the sound of Asa's shoes at the door with an inspector who counts. Either way, the ink has spoken in a way even Daria's crowd can learn.

CHAPTER 11

Blade Nick

Lunch crowd drifted out with tote bags and paperbacks, the sort of steady trade that keeps lights on and tempers even. Miss Dotty held the front ledger like a hymnal. Rafi boxed two online orders with the care of a man who knows tape has a memory. Peppermint guarded the sun patch on the carpet with the surly joy of a small emperor.

The bell chimed and brought in citrus and camera flash. Daria Lin crossed the threshold as if she owned the floor. White jacket, a touch of gold at the throat, polite sunglasses parked in her hair. Her smile tried to make our shop a branch office of her club.

"Liora," she sang. "Tell me you have triumph news for tonight."

"News," I said. "Triumph belongs to hard facts."

She set her phone on the counter as if that made us partners. The screen showed a draft caption with my shop's handle preloaded. Her thumb nick had lost its blush, still fresh, a peel catching at the edge. Concealer masked the worst of it, matte with a faint pink cast.

"You asked for the list," she said. "We sent a digest at noon. VIPs hidden until six. Surprise intact."

"You sent a headline, not a list," I said. "Names and times are still missing. Send the log or Asa will count heads with the city by two."

She weighed whether to spar. Not today. She slid the phone back to her palm. "I came to be gracious," she said. "A touch of goodwill between neighbors. Your crowd trusts you. Let me host the reveal and we both eat."

"Eat what," Miss Dotty said, mild as tea.

"Attention," Daria said. "Attention spends."

"Attention spends and then asks for change," Miss Dotty said, then returned to her ledger.

I kept my eyes on Daria's hands. Right thumb curved in, tender at the side. Call it stage damage. Call it box work. Either way, I wanted to see what she did with paper when the room forgot her.

"Help me with a quick flip," I said. "House request. A donor asked if the jacket hides a tear."

I placed a midcentury hardcover on the felt. Blue cloth, cream jacket, deckle fore edge that honest printers leave alone. The jacket sat tight along the spine, a clean fit. I rotated the book so the fore edge faced her. Habit test.

She reached with both hands and pinched the deckles between thumb and index. Right thumb set on top, angled down and across the grain, the exact rake that would slice skin if a blade skipped. Her left kept the pressure steady while her right made the work. She pulled the fore edge toward her and used the pinch to open the boards.

"Careful," I said.

She paused, then smiled like a teacher who forgives a slow pupil. "I handle books every day," she said.

"You handle rooms," I said. "Books require a different grip."

She kept the pinch. She lifted the jacket corner and skimmed under with the same right-hand thumb that wore a peel. The pad grazed the paper at the exact corner I planned to watch.

"See," she said. "Gentle. I could work at your desk."

"Not with that pinch," I said. "Fore edges want support from the spine, not a pinch at the deckle. You press there and you train the fibers to roll. A knife learns that angle if you teach it often enough."

She laughed, small and bright. "You make everything a sermon."

I let her turn two more leaves. Same grip. Same angle. Same hurry disguised as poise. The peel on her thumb kissed the jacket's corner and left a shadow the color of warm sand. A trace of silicone slip caught the light. Concealer. The smear was no larger than a sesame seed.

I held my breath and watched it settle. She pressed again. A second whisper of color landed on the board under the jacket flap, a line too faint for anyone but a person who counts fibers.

"Looks good," she said. "No tear. You can tell your donor she saved a bit of value by not tossing the jacket in a spring purge."

She closed the book and set it down with the same pinch, thumb riding the edge. The peel bent. Her face did not flicker. People who love a stage train their skin to behave.

"Thank you," I said. "You helped."

"I do that," she said. "Mutuals keep a city kind."

She turned, took two steps toward the table where last night's intake sat in a neat stack for catalog. Her hand drifted across the top jacket like a dragonfly. The corner lifted and settled. I saw the faintest blush of the same warm sand mark kiss that jacket too. I marked the corner in my head and kept my face still.

"Cute run of jackets," she said. "You snag these at auction."

"Estate," Rafi said. "Neighbor with good taste and a label maker."

"You keep secrets better than I do," she said, then faced me again. "So. Tonight. The reveal at The Bindery. What time suits you."

"Never," I said.

She blinked once, then smiled wider, the way a person does when a waiter tells them the caviar is out. "You are funny."

"I am working," I said. "Your reveal belongs in a room with

newer chairs."

She glanced at Miss Dotty, then at the case light as if it might soften me. "You cannot freeze the city to protect your mood," she said.

"You cannot sell pageant in place of proof," I said.

She tried a different angle. "Let me host your note about provenance. My crowd loves process. Your test strips, your lamps, the things you do with water and patience. We can bring that to light and then pivot to the first."

"You pivot to first," I said. "I walk to the next step in line."

She set her phone on the counter again and let the screen glow with my handle. "Be practical," she said. "You bring truth. I bring heat. The book gets a better buyer. Everyone wins."

I reached under the counter, took out a small swab kit, and unwrapped a single sterile tip. I held it up and met her eyes. "Do not move."

"Excuse me," she said.

"Concealer on the corner," I said. "I am lifting it for the file. It is makeup, not a stain. It will bag clean. You can watch."

She looked down at the book she had flipped and then at the intake stack. Her smile lost a tooth. "You cannot take my face and put it in your folder," she said.

"I will take residue from a jacket corner," I said. "It becomes a marker for who touched what and when. If I never need it, it sleeps in a bag forever."

"That feels invasive," she said.

"Not more than a blind spot in a lot," I said.

She held still. I touched the swab to the jacket corner she had kissed with the peel. The tip picked up a whisper of color that read warm sand on white. I dotted a control square on a card and the swab left a small quarter-moon. I took a quick photo with today's paper in frame, then slid the swab into a microtube and labeled it with time, title, and corner A.

"Chain," Miss Dotty said without looking up. I read the line to her. She wrote it down and signed.

I lifted the jacket from the intake stack and swabbed that corner too. The tip bloomed faint pink again. Two matches. I bagged both and sealed the microtubes with a strip of tape that I signed and dated. Rafi held the trash so I did not break my line.

Daria watched the tape pull tight, then looked back at my face. "You are a machine," she said, less kind.

"You asked for practical," I said.

She picked up the midcentury book again and touched the fore edge with a more careful grip. Her thumb still wanted the corner. Training runs deep. She fought it and lost. The peel grazed the card on the counter. A small dot of concealer sat on the cardstock like a tiny moon. I slid the card into the bin for contaminated service waste without speaking.

"Is this theater," she said. "You are making me feel like a suspect in my own city."

"Agents of spectacle survive that feeling," I said. "You will be fine."

Peppermint stretched and sauntered across the counter as if to break the wire between us. Daria scratched his chin. He endured it with the patience of a saint who expects tribute. Her thumb brushed his collar. He wiggled, shed a hair, and hopped down with a thump.

"See," she said. "We can be friends."

"We can be clear," I said.

She stood straighter. "Tell me what you want," she said.

"Names with times," I said. "Door counts per hour. Key logs for the storeroom. Camera map with retention. Clip of your hands on the case."

"Second list arrives at four," she said. "Key logs by six. Cameras we do not share without counsel."

"Counsel can read," I said.

She glanced toward the window, read the street, set her phone on the counter for the third time. She likes props. "You do know I can bury you online," she said, smile neat, voice soft. "One story about an old shop that fumbled a once-in-a-century chance and my crowd will eat you for sport."

Miss Dotty closed the ledger. The sound was small and absolute. "One story about a club that hugged a forged margin and the museum people will stop taking your calls," she said, eyes on Daria as if they were the only two in the room.

Daria's smile cracked, then reset. "You cannot prove that," she said.

I tapped the evidence tray under the case light. The strip from this morning glowed like a firm no. "We can," I said. "We did."

Her jaw worked once. She let it go. "Fine," she said. "You win today."

"This is not a game," I said.

She turned to leave, then pivoted back for one more shot at charm. "When can I host the reveal," she asked, soft, perfect, eyes bright with stage rain.

"Never," I said.

Silence took the counter for a clean count of three. She held my eyes, then put on her sunglasses indoors like a person who thinks glass is a force field.

"You will come around," she said.

I waited.

She left with that citrus trail and a door swing that drew eyes from the street. The bell sighed and settled.

Rafi exhaled first. "I liked the part where you did not blink," he said.

"I save blinking for smoke," I said.

Peppermint jumped back to the sun patch and flopped, untroubled by city wars.

I lifted the jacket from the intake stack with gloved hands, slid a clean interleave into the corner, and wrote a note for the file. Warm sand concealer, silicone base, two lifts from two objects touched within five minutes. Right thumb peel still fresh.

Miss Dotty set the ledger at my elbow. "Blade floated," she said.

"It floats," I said. "We wait to name the hand that used it. She did not need help with that."

Rafi brought the bagged microtubes for my signature. I signed, dated, and added the case number that now holds more truth than she wants. The phone buzzed. Asa, short and on time.

Asa: Got the noon nothing. Ink added. Send any lift docs. Afternoon call holds.

I texted him a photo of the tubes beside today's paper and the case light, then the note about the deckle pinch and the angle. He answered with one word that landed like a nail.

Copy.

I put the midcentury book back on the felt and breathed the slow breath you take when a stubborn knot starts to loosen. Daria clung to first like a talisman. First does not bless poor hands. Paper remembers touch even when faces forget.

CHAPTER 12

Press Visit

The old press room sits three blocks south of the river, brick stained by a century of steam and ink. A painted sign still clings to the lintel, gold flaking off a serif R. Inside, it smells like oil, paper dust, and long days. Iron hulks rest on skids, flywheels locked, rollers wrapped in brown craft paper like sleeping arms. A fan ticks in the corner and moves warm air in circles.

Len Carter waits at a workbench with a mug that reads Keep Fair Register. His hair is a close gray brush, his hands square, his shirt clean in a way only pressmen manage. I met him once when we hunted a counterfeit club program with a fake sponsor line. He liked our chain. He liked that I spoke in dates.

"You picked a good day," he says. "The boys cleared the proof room, so the files are easy."

"Bless your files," I say. "I need a grid from the year in question. Full sheet, not a promo sliver."

"You mean the dot grid, not the halftone," he says. "Registration alignment, not a screen."

"Dot grid," I say. "Clean, with measurements. I want a match or a miss."

He takes a key from a nail and lifts a gate on a short run of shelves. Brown folders sit in neat rows, labels written in an old hand with a stubby pencil. He pulls one marked with the year and a month. He opens it with care, palms flat, breath steady.

"Sample sheet," he says. "Pulled after the makeready, signed by me, kept flat. We kept one for every job that mattered."

He spreads the sheet on the bench and weights the corners with little lead pigs in the shape of birds. The paper glows cream under the bench lamp. A faint lattice of hairline dots sits in the margins, four up, two across, each dot tied to a tiny figure that marks position. Not ornaments. Not dirt. A map.

"Look here," Len says, tapping a dot near the tail of the sheet. "Grid set. We used this house scheme for three seasons. Every frame hung off this pattern. If the printer drifted, dots would tell the story."

"Distance from head," I say.

"Forty-six and a half," he says without a ruler. He reaches for one anyway, checks, nods. "Forty-six and a half. Left gutter sits at twelve on this line, right at thirty-eight. Numbers live in my fingers."

I take a photo with today's paper in frame, then another with a clear shot of the dots near the colophon area. He watches me work and seems pleased by the lack of drama.

"You brought me a book last year," he says. "Had a registration cross near the foot you liked."

"Different case," I say. "Same need."

He lifts a loupe from his pocket and peers at the lower left. "Dot here, dot here," he says. "Sharp. No plate wear. Journal says the plate was fresh, no re-run."

"Plate notes," I say.

He opens a second folder and pulls a card with grease pencil marks. "Two pulls to lock ink. Third to lock feed. Walter ran the feed that week."

"Walter Mott," I say. "Worked under you."

"He ran as a sub when we needed him," Len says. "Good with hands, better with talk. Knew how to calm a donor who wanted an early look. Also liked side jobs."

"Side jobs," I say.

He grins like a man with a memory he enjoys in private. "Walter liked helping friends for cash. Sometimes that meant a late-night skid to a sponsor who cried about a gala. Sometimes it meant a garage bind for a club piece that lost a jacket. Always a little off the books, always with a smile. He saw himself as a patron saint of tight deadlines."

"You knew he worked off-site."

"I knew he drove a van with no name on the door," Len says. "I knew his garage had a heater in winter and a rack for boards. I knew I should not ask questions if the main job was in on time and the numbers matched."

He points to the grid again and taps a spot near the spine fold. "That your trouble spot," he asks. "Right here near the tail fold. Dot sits here on the real thing. Some of the copies I have seen in the wild show a dot that rides high, or a dot that sits soft like a tired stamp."

I take my phone from my pocket and open the case photo. I zoom to the place where our dot sits like a drunk at a choir rail. He squints and makes a sound in his teeth.

"High by a mill," he says. "Not a press drift. Not on our line. If you showed me this in a blind, I would say a second body laid in a piece or a repair went wrong."

"Dot grid from the year says clean. Our copy says off," I say.

"Yup," he says. "If you want me polite, I would call it wrong. If you want me honest, I would call it swapped."

I write both words in my notebook, then take a measurement from his sheet and write it beside my photo measurement. Len reads upside down with ease.

"You want a house sample to show a judge," he says. "I can give you a copy stamped sample, not the original. Original lives here. Photo holds up better anyway."

"Photo with your signature and the date on the folder," I say. "You in frame."

He sets the sheet again, places his hand with the grease pencil card near the bottom, and looks up at me with that square pressman smile. I take three shots. One wide, one medium, one macro of the dot and the number key. Then I take one more of the folder label and his hand on the edge.

He lifts the sheet and slips it back into the folder like a priest bedding a relic. He locks the gate again and hangs the key.

"You have the dot grid," he says. "You have my word on the measure. You want more meat, you find out who trimmed or laid in a new piece."

"Trim," I say. "Deckle talk helps. Walter's name sits on the week. He worked a side rack that year. You saw him bring boards to the garage."

He shrugs, not shy, only careful. "I saw boards leave the back door under his arm," he says. "I did not see them come back unless a job needed a quick fix nobody signed for. Boys tried to keep me innocent. I am not that innocent."

"Anyone else run side favors," I ask.

"Everyone helps someone," he says. "Walter helped more. Club managers loved him. He drank their gin and called them by first name. People like that think rules bend for charm."

He walks to a shelf and pulls a ledger book. He flips to the week we need and taps a margin note. "W. M. night assist," it reads in pencil. No money listed beside it, only a small tick that Len says he used to mark favors outside the clock. He shows me a run of ticks for a six-month span. Walter's column runs heavy.

"What did he assist," I ask.

"Anything with a loose hinge," he says. "Cases that squeaked. Jackets that needed a new fold. Donor sheets that wanted trimming in a hurry so a patron could wave them at dinner. He liked knives. Said a sharp blade kept lies neat."

"Knife talk fits today," I say.

He glances at my face. "You found a cut."

"On a thumb," I say. "Right hand. Concealer this morning over a peel. Angle reads trim work in haste."

"Who wears concealer," he asks with a smile that knows the answer.

"House host," I say.

"Then she handled a knife or a tape pull," he says. "It happens. Hosts think tape is clean, pull wrong, blade slides, thumb pays."

I look over the room. Plates hang on the wall, little squares of etched metal from tourist jobs. The big cylinder press sits with a stripe of light across its bed. The air holds the weight of machines that do one thing and do it well.

"Tell me about dot grids," I say. "Explain in plain words for a jury that wants pictures."

Len nods and picks up a pencil stub. He draws a rectangle, then a set of little dots along the long edge, then numbers near them. "Every pressman needs a way to check position," he says. "We use tiny dots that line up with a frame only we know. It looks like dirt to normal eyes. To us it is a map. If a sheet gets cut wrong or a piece is lifted and laid again, dots tell on you. They will sit high or low, or they will soften because a second impression never kisses the same."

"Your year kept this exact map."

"For that title and that plate," he says. "We kept it consistent, because donors pay for neatness and you cannot sell neatness if your marks dance."

"You have a sample from a different run," I ask. "Another title from the same house that season."

He pulls a second folder and opens it. Same grid. Same measures. He lets me shoot those dots as well. "Consistency is a religion," he says. "If I had a boy drift, he bought lunch and listened to me tell him why he was wrong."

"Walter bought lunch often," I say.

"He charmed the room into buying lunch for him," Len says. "Which is different."

"Tell me about Walter's garage."

Len scratches his jaw and looks at the door like a man who counts who walks by in case a cousin shows up with a complaint. "He runs it in the back of his semi-detached near the canal," he says. "Door painted green. No sign. You want a number."

"I have one," I say. "Asa pulled a registry when we wrote the first memo."

Len smiles. "You boys write memos," he says with affection. "Good. Bring a light. He keeps poor bulbs in there. He keeps boxes stacked taller than sense. He keeps a table heavy with knives that look like he took them to bed."

"Ever seen donor sheets in his van," I ask.

"Yes," Len says, no hesitation. "Brown around the edge from bad storage. We told the club to keep those in a cold room. They stored them under a bar. Walter hauled a set out for a sponsor dinner where somebody wanted to look clever and pin one under a lamp."

"Acid halos," I say.

"Exactly," he says. "You warm a sheet with acid in the size and any fool can see the edge glow. Donors clap because brown reads old to them. It reads poor practice to me."

"Did Walter know better."

"He knew better," Len says. "He also knew what sponsors clap for, and he preferred clapping to rules."

I take a breath and look back at the sample sheet. The dots read like a straight ruler. Our copy reads like a bent one. A clean, safe claim.

"Do you want a statement," Len asks. "I can write one on

letterhead before my nap."

"Yes," I say. "One paragraph. Grid for this title and plate sits as marked on your sample. Our copy's grid sits high by one mill. Conclusion reads mismatch."

He writes with that stub, neat block letters in the voice of a man who has signed off on more runs than I have eaten breakfasts. He dates it, signs, and adds his old title under his name. I take a photo with today's paper, then slip the original into a sleeve and seal it. He nods at my tape and signs across it with a flourish he likely reserves for moments when a room respects his trade.

We walk past the cylinder press on the way out. He puts his hand on the bed as if he can still feel heat there. He probably can.

"Walter runs hot," Len says as if reading my outline. "He likes rooms with clapping and smoke. He likes side doors. He will tell you he saves the day. Sometimes he did. Other times he saved himself."

"Who else worked beside him on that week," I ask.

"Gina on ink," he says. "Ray on feed for the morning shift, Walter on feed for the night. Marta counted sheets, Denby did plates, I signed the rack. If you ask Gina about gels in margins, she will tell you no in a voice that sings."

"She hates modern ink on old pages."

"She hates lies," he says. "Ink is the tool."

He stops at a pegboard and lifts a thin metal rule with tiny holes along one edge. "Take this with you," he says. "Old straightedge with pin points. Pressmen use it to check dot positions without leaving marks. Good for photographs beside a trouble spot. I have spares."

"I will return it," I say.

"Keep it," he says. "Call it a present for people who keep their heads when a club rings a bell."

I bag the rule in a clear sleeve, write a label, and tuck it into my case. He walks me to the door and looks out at the street like a man watching weather.

"You asked for a place to look," he says. "I pointed once. I will point again. Walter's garage. If I were a person with a knife and a taste for applause, I would do my fixes where nobody interrupts me. If anything from your trouble book was lifted, fixed, or swapped, the board that held it sat on his table at some point."

"Thank you," I say.

"Wear boots," he says. "Oil on concrete never forgives pretty shoes."

"Keys for a safe visit," I ask.

"Drop by near dinner when boys want food," he says. "He talks more with a plate in front of him. Bring coffee for Gina if you want a friend for life. She lives two doors down and hates noise."

I shake his hand. He squeezes mine with the calm pressure of a man who knows force in his sleep but only uses it when bolts rust. He goes back to his bench and his birds of lead, and I step into the late light.

On the walk back I send Asa two photos. Sample sheet with dots and Len's signature. Len at the bench with the folder, date legible. I add one line. Grid clean, ours off by one mill. Len confirms Walter on night feed that week. Walter's habit of side favors, garage table with knives.

He replies in under a minute. Added to file. Garage goes top of the hour after we press the club.

I text Rafi. Pull the small flashlight and the nitrile. Tell Miss Dotty we will be out for an hour after two.

Rafi answers with a thumbs-up emoji that never sits in our evidence but always sits well in my head.

At the corner, a bus sighs and lets out a pair of students who both carry blue tote bags with university logos. Salt prickles my scalp. Blue tote, thin elbows, gel-slicked hair. The echo in my notes steps forward. Not proof, only a shape that matches the edges.

Back at the shop I set Len's statement under glass and tape the rule to the board with a label. Dot grid anchored. I print a single sheet for our binder with three points that a jury can carry. Year's grid sits here. Our copy sits there. Difference equals lay-in or trim outside house practice.

Peppermint jumps onto the counter and stares at the photo of the old press as if it smells like warm metal through the paper. Miss Dotty reads Len's paragraph and nods once.

"He points you again," she says.

"He does," I say. "Walter's garage."

She closes the ledger and slides me a small tin. Inside sit two sugar mints and a folded ten for the inevitable cash-only coffee. I take both.

"Be kind," she says. "Be firm. Watch for knives."

"I like rooms with rules," I say.

"We build one wherever we stand," she says.

The bell rings. A regular asks for a mystery with a train and a train schedule. Rafi handles it with a smile that makes tips appear. I check the clock. Two sits close. Time to stop nibbling and bite.

Old dots told me where honest work lives. Our copy lies in the trivial measure by a mill. A mill is a world when a room wants truth. Len Carter gave me a handhold and a door. Both point one direction.

Walter's garage again.

CHAPTER 13

Car Trunk

The call came as I shelved a fresh stack of paperbacks. Asa first, short and sharp.

"Hospital lot. South wing. They found a seller in a trunk. Alive."

"Name."

"Marin Grove. Shop invoices under Grove Fine Ephemera. Blue tote in half our witness notes."

"I am five minutes away," I said.

Rafi grabbed the small field kit before I asked. Miss Dotty slipped the ledger into the safe and locked it with a click that anchored my spine.

"Boots," she said. "Gloves. Calm voice."

We hit the street. Air held that iron smell a city gets when rain threatens but does not show. Sirens somewhere else. Horns. Shoes. The usual.

The hospital lot sat behind a beige block with windows that did not care about anyone's mood. Tape fluttered at one aisle. Two security guards made a human gate. DI Jude Havel stood with his arms folded and a bottle of water he did not drink. Clean coat. Tired eyes that still paid attention.

"Thank you for moving," he said. "We pulled her at one forty-eight. Breathing. Pulse slow but steady. She met a buyer at noon, moved again at one for a second look. Ended up in the trunk by one thirty."

"Lured," I said.

"Text thread says so," he said. "Language reads club-adjacent. VIP wants private peek near the ward. Sick relative as reason to pick this lot."

"Books," I said.

"Back seat," he said, and led me to a silver hatchback idling under cloud light. Rear door left ajar. On the seat sat two jackets I knew from last night's intake list. Under those, a cloth-wrapped bundle she had not placed yet. Protective foam on the floor. A blue tote on its side, logo faded by bad washing.

"Trunk," Havel said, and looked to the forensic tech at the rear for permission.

White tape marked a square on the lip where they had lifted a print. The inner lip showed a scuff, fresh enough to reflect morning light. At the edge of the scuff sat a pale smear, warm beige with a faint silicone sheen. No dust stuck to it. Concealer reads smooth even when grime tries to cling.

"Fresh," I said.

"Hour at most," the tech said. "No glitter, no shimmer. Matte with slip."

I did not say the color's name out loud. Warm sand. It sat in my mind like a bell.

"Where did they find her," I asked.

"In here," Havel said. "Fetal curl, hands tied with packing tape, gag loose from a bad knot. Whoever did it wanted speed. They did not want blood."

"Any sign of a blade," I asked.

"Clean cut on tape tails. No tool on scene," he said. "Right-hand work from the angle of the tails and how they sit. I saw enough to be sure."

I looked at the scuff again. The smear sat where a thumb would push down on the lip to snap the trunk shut with the natural hook and press. Same angle as a deckle pinch, same angle as a hasty trim, same risk to a right-hand thumb that forgot to stop near metal.

"Marin," I said, looking at the EMTs through the windshield.

"Conscious, on oxygen, answering to her name," Havel said. "We will talk when she clears more fog."

Two security officers rolled a monitor to us. Inside the booth a guard in a sweater vest tapped keys and squinted.

"Camera two, south aisle, one twenty-seven to one forty," the vest said. "No audio. It stutters when the wind hits the pole."

He hit play and we watched the line of cars shimmer. Marin's hatchback pulled in at one twenty-eight. She stepped out with a careful body, one hand on her tote, eyes on her phone. Short jacket, jeans, hair up in a clip. She checked her screen. She looked toward the entrance, then toward the row of trees by the wall.

A figure stepped into frame at one thirty-two from the far side, walking fast, phone to ear, head high as if the world took instructions from that angle. Height near mine, maybe a touch shorter in those shoes. Shape under a bright jacket that read white to the camera, a gold flash at the throat catching light once, twice.

The figure raised a hand in greeting without a wave. Marin smiled, relaxed her shoulders, slid the tote onto the back seat. The two spoke for a count of five with a lot of space between words. The figure pointed toward the trees, then to the car. Marin reached into the front seat for a small cloth-wrapped bundle. The figure leaned into the open trunk, checking space. Marin moved closer. A bump of shoulders, then the quick two-step of someone losing balance and someone else guiding that fall. The figure's hand pressed the inner lip for leverage. The hand slipped toward the edge as the trunk came down.

The feed stuttered. A frame jumped.

Next frame, trunk shut. The figure stood close, head tipped down, checking the seam. A small shift, then the figure reached across to wipe the edge with a thumb and a square of tissue. Finger made a small circle on the lip, then the figure stepped back, pulled the rear door, and placed the cloth-wrapped bundle on the seat. A glance up toward the camera. A swipe of hair at the temple. A turn on the heel. Walk away.

No one else in range.

Havel paused the frame where the hand pressed the lip.

"Clean enough for a print," he said.

"Or at least a lift for product match," I said. "Concealer swab, silicone carrier, warm sand base."

"Your new favorite color," he said.

I did not answer. The guard hit play again. A nurse with a lunch bag walked into frame and then out. A pair of med students crossed behind the hatchback, blind to everything. At one forty-eight a hospital security cart rolled in with a guard already on the radio.

"How did they find her," I asked.

"Nurse walked by, heard a thump," Havel said. "She thought it was the spare tire banging, then she heard a foot. She hits the call button that talks to the booth and we move."

"Who called Marin," I said.

Havel pulled his notepad and read. "Unknown number with a club-affiliated area code," he said. "Content: VIP, sick relative, needs comfort of a small win before a hard visit. Words smell like a host who thinks mercy is set dressing. Meet at south lot. Bring the real one for a thirty-second peep. Cash on return for discretion."

"Her reply," I said.

"On my way. Two copies in car. One is best," he said. "Then a short line with a question mark. She asked who uses this phrasing. No answer."

"Who else saw," I asked.

"Nurse with the lunch bag saw a white jacket near the hatch, but did not clock a face," he said. "Said perfume read citrus. She hates orange so she noticed."

"Citrus and camera frame make a chorus," I said.

"Do not sing yet," Havel said. "Names later. For now, you stand here and tell me what else your book eyes see before I let the techs swab."

I leaned in without crossing tape. The back seat told a clean story. Books were intact, corners crisp, jackets clean. She had planned to show and tell without opening too far. On the floor, foam cutouts for a safe fit sat like a puzzle, missing one piece from the slot nearest the door. No smear on those. On the mat near the right rear footwell, one grain of orange peel. Fresh scent, not baked. The car still held a ghost of breakfast and cold air, not smoke.

"Orange," I said, and pointed with a gloved finger so the tech could collect it.

"Picked," the tech said, and opened a small vial.

"Phone charger plugged in, seat back set, driver's mirror high," I said. "She expected a quick return."

The tote on the seat had one broken strap. Stitch gave near a prior repair. The logo, a university crest, sat half-peeled. The zipper pull bore a scuff that looked like a ring had hit it in a hurry.

"Ring," I said.

"Right-hand ring in the social photo," Rafi said. He had stood silent to that point, eyes on the details, hands to himself. He pointed to the zipper pull and then to the lift point at the trunk. Same arc, same kind of split-second hit.

"Books never left the back seat," I said. "No one dug through. She was the target, not the stock."

"Or the stock was bait," Havel said. "Real aim, the seller."

"Who called her knows panic and grace," I said. "They lined two things in a row. A sick relative and a VIP. One trick to pull empathy, one to pull greed."

"Seller profiles fit both," Havel said. "She likes money, she likes myths. She also likes feeling helpful."

He looked at the EMTs again. "She will tell me the middle once the fog burns off."

"Camera on the north corner," I said, pointing to a pole near the trees. "Angle on the other side of the hatch."

"Dead," the guard said. "Shakes in wind, loop breaks. We need a part."

"Every blind spot in this city needs a part," Havel said, tired and calm.

I photographed the car with today's paper tucked at the edge of the windshield where it could not step on evidence. The tech shot the same frame with scale cards lined along the lip. I made a short voice note for Asa while Havel stepped away to talk to a nurse who had shown up with a clipboard and a stubborn chin.

"Hospital lot, south wing. Marin Grove lured by club text. Books intact in back seat. Marin found in trunk, tape on hands. Concealer smear on trunk lip. Right-hand press. Camera shows a figure near Marin's height in a white jacket with a gold flash at the throat. Thumb wipes the lip with tissue before walk-off. Rafi noted ring scuff on zipper. Orange peel on mat. Swabs and lifts underway."

Asa sent one word: Copy.

Rafi looked at me the way he does when a knot begins to show its form. "She got the same pitch I have heard a hundred times," he said. "Make a gift to fix a day. Help a stranger. Be part of a story."

"Hosts who sell a story never stop at one tool," I said. "They stack them."

The EMTs loaded Marin onto a stretcher and moved toward the south doors. A young doc met them, steady and kind. Marin's eyes opened, then closed again. A string of hair had fallen out of her clip and stuck to her cheek with sweat.

"Family coming," Havel said. "We will wait an hour, then try for ten words that matter."

A black sedan rolled in on the far side of the lot. Asa stepped out and walked with a litigator's pace that tells you shoes matter. He took in the tape and the camera and made a short circuit before he reached us.

"Cameras keep hurting my feelings," he said. "They never point where the stories happen."

"They point where the budget allows," Havel said. "And the wind decides the rest."

Asa nodded at the trunk lip. "Concealer," he said.

"Warm sand," I said.

He did not smile. "And a silicone carrier," he said. "I will write it so a judge reads it and cares. We will match it to a swab from your lifts if we need to. Either way, we lock the angle. Right-hand press at the lip."

"Your noon file helped," Havel said. "Ink is modern. Now time is short."

Asa watched the feed on the small screen while the guard scruffed at the monitor like it might reveal a cleaner frame.

"She took a wipe to the edge," he said. "People who stage scenes always over-clean where eyes go first. They forget cameras like the sides."

"White jacket," Havel said. "Gold flash at the throat. Height and stride near our host."

"We do not speak names yet," Asa said. "We speak lines and angles. But yes. The outline reads familiar."

My phone buzzed. Miss Dotty. I stepped away to take it.

"Are you steady," she said.

"I am," I said. "Marin alive. Books safe. Concealer on trunk. Camera frame with a bright jacket. Orange peel on mat."

"Bring back a copy of the still if you can, no faces. I want it for the board," she said. "Also, the museum called to say hello. They read your morning memo and offered a preservation tech for loan. They smell smoke."

"Good," I said. "Tell them we will take help once Havel clears scene work."

Rafi rejoined me with a printout from the booth. The guard had popped a still and sent it to the small printer. He handed me a copy and then passed one to Havel.

"Frame one thirty-two, hand on lip," he said. "Scaled to license plate width."

The still froze the hand mid-press. The jacket sleeve sat crisp and bright. A gold flash at the throat reflected near the car window like a tiny sun. The figure's face sat out of range, which was a gift for now.

I took a pen and marked the dot grid tattoo in my mind where the pressman had set his marks. The camera gave me a similar overlay to measure. I wrote the plate width on the back and the time and the camera number.

"Marin will hate me," I said. "She will hate that her best copy pulled this much mud to her name."

"Her best copy got her into the trunk," Asa said. "Your work will get her out of trouble."

Havel looked up at the sky and then back at the car. "We are done here for now," he said to the tech. "Swabs, prints, lifts, then tow. I want it under a roof by four."

"On it," the tech said.

We stood by the curb while the team did their hands-first dance. Havel's phone chirped and he read in silence for ten seconds, then handed it to me.

"Marin's texts from the last hour," he said. "She gave consent for a pull. Her hands were taped, not her phone."

On the screen: unknown number with a location pin near the

south lot. Then the line that made my teeth touch. Bring the good one. Quick peek only. VIP needs it.

Rafi read over my shoulder. "Term of art," he said. "Good one."

"No one outside our trade uses that phrase without guidance," I said.

Asa nodded once, sparse as ever. "You will tell me later whether the phrase shows up in any of our host's prior posts," he said. "For now, we take it as one more piece on one side of the board."

Havel pocketed the phone. "You go back to the shop," he said to me. "Keep your chain tidy. I will call when Marin has three sentences for you. Do not let your host steamroll you before sunset."

"She wanted a reveal tonight," I said.

"She can ask a wall," he said.

We walked back to the car. A gust brought citrus to nose level and then it was gone, carried across the lot and into the block as if the city refused to hold it.

Rafi drove so I could send Asa the still and my notes. I wrote them in short lines that a judge would not trip over.

• Seller found in trunk at 1:48 p.m., south hospital lot. Alive, taped, no blood.

• Books intact on back seat. No rummage. Stock used as bait.

• Trunk lip shows fresh scuff with warm beige concealer smear, silicone slip. Right-hand press angle.

• Camera 2 shows figure near seller's height in bright jacket with gold flash at throat. Hand presses lip and wipes with tissue before leaving.

• Orange peel on right rear mat. Nurse smelled citrus near hatch.

• Text lure from unknown number, club-adjacent area code. Phrases include "VIP" and "good one." Seller replied, "On my way," referenced two copies, one best.

Asa replied in seconds. Added to file. Ink, dots, trunk, text. The board for this case can now walk on its own.

At the light, Rafi glanced over. "Time to stop dancing around her," he said.

"We float, we do not accuse," I said. "We press on logs and clips and who was where when. We let her hear the part about warm sand on metal. People who live for rooms always think rooms will save them."

He snorted. "Rooms do not vote in court."

Back at the shop Miss Dotty had already taped a new card to the board. Hospital lot, south wing. Under it she had clipped the still Rafi printed and left space for one more below it. She moved the gel strip photo to the left and drew a line to the still with a pencil in a clean arc.

"Marin," she said.

"Will talk soon," I said. "She got the old mercy bait."

"Who sent the text," she asked.

"Number unknown, club area code," I said. "Language reads close to our host. Good one as a phrase. VIP as seasoning."

Miss Dotty did not say the name, same as me. She touched the edge of the still with a finger and then sat. "You will go to the garage," she said. "Do not let the tools distract you."

Rafi lifted the field kit again and set a roll of nitrile on top.

"Before we go," I said, "I want you to see this."

I set the printed still beside the trunk-lip swab photos from earlier and the shot of Daria's thumb nick from this morning. Concealer color matched in the way color lives in a person's eye. Warm sand in three scenes. I wrote it on a card but wrote it as observation, not as charge.

The shop bell chimed. The world wanted a slim novel where someone lies and someone pays and no one gets in a trunk.

We took a breath, long and steady. The phone buzzed. Havel again.

"Security pulled one more angle," he said. "West wing entrance camera picks up the walk-away. Frame is bad, but height and line match the white jacket. I will bring the clip for your board once my tech signs chain."

He paused. "I know you prefer language to fire, Wren, but I want this on the record. Whoever staged that trunk wanted fear without risk. A thing like that escalates fast in a city with cameras hooked to broken poles."

"I hear you," I said.

He exhaled into the line. "Good. Keep your head. Pull your boots. I will meet you at the garage after I speak to Marin."

I hung up and looked at the still again. The hand pressed the lip. The smear sat where light could see it, where a tidy mind would try to hide it, where a camera took its time and told the truth.

Peppermint thumped his tail against the window frame as if a pigeon had spoken out of turn.

"Urgency raised," Miss Dotty said, reading my face.

"It is," I said. "Our seller survived a trunk. Our club wants a reveal. Our board has a hand on metal and a product with a name."

Rafi picked up the keys.

"Garage," he said.

"Garage," I said.

The phone buzzed one more time. A message from the hospital guard's booth. Security had packaged the clip. A single line preview sat above the link.

Figure approaches hatch, size and stride match Daria Lin.

CHAPTER 14

Meet in the Stacks

We did not head straight to Walter's garage. First we locked the meet.

The alley behind Peppermint Cat runs narrow as a book gutter, brick on one side, our back door and two bins on the other. A small dome camera sits above our shop light. It feeds to a recorder under the counter that Rafi treats like a small god. If the city ever tries to tell a story with confetti instead of timestamps, our alley keeps the grammar honest.

Rafi pulled the monitor to the worktable while Miss Dotty set out the chain cards. I closed the blinds on the back door so sun would not wash the screen. Peppermint hopped onto the chair beside me and faced the monitor like a tiny auditor.

"Day before yesterday," I said. "Dusk. Twenty before the club posted time. Run until full dark."

Rafi logged in, fingers quick. He scrubbed the timeline. The alley flickered to life. Pigeons held committee on the bins. Two kids rolled past on scooters. Nothing for a while. Then at 18:07 a frame shift, a head of hair I knew, a blue tote I had met twice in two days.

"Freeze," I said.

Rafi froze. Marin Grove stepped into frame from the street end.

Jacket zipped. Tote on shoulder. Phone in her left hand, thumb moving. She paused under the camera and looked at our sign as if reading the cat's name would steady her.

"Time mark," Miss Dotty said.

I read the overlay. "Eighteen oh seven twelve."

Rafi rolled it forward one second at a time. Marin pinned her phone under her chin and retied the tote strap. She checked the street. She checked the side lot gate. She stood in the spill of our light and breathed once like a runner at the line.

At 18:08 a second figure entered from the opposite direction, bright jacket that read white to the sensor, a gold flash at the throat that caught our light for half a beat. Chin high. Phone in hand. Daria.

"Freeze," I said again.

Rafi froze on a clean frame where the two women looked at each other without touching. Daria raised a hand to shoulder height, not a wave, a claim on the space. Marin answered with her shoulder dropping out of its knot. The tote strap slid a fraction.

"Time," Miss Dotty said.

"Eighteen oh eight twenty-nine," I read.

Rafi let it roll. Daria stepped closer and showed her screen. Marin read it and nodded. Daria tilted her head at the side lot and took a single step back, not forward, the signal of a person who expects the other to follow. Marin did. They moved toward the gate with their shoulders almost touching but not quite. At the corner, Daria turned to the camera for a fraction, not by accident. People who live for rooms always play to the back row.

The two fell out of frame at 18:09:02. Rafi rolled ten seconds more and hit stop. The empty alley looked innocent again.

I did not speak for a full count of five. Then I let my breath out.

"We bag stills," I said. "Wide on approach, medium on meet, tight on the gold flash."

"Chain," Miss Dotty said.

I read it off as Rafi printed the frames. We slid each print into a sleeve with a card that carried time and overlay source. I took one shot of the monitor with today's paper propped in the corner for the file, then closed the clip and wrote the hash onto the card. Peppermint flicked an ear and approved.

"Run the side lot camera," I said.

"We do not own it," Rafi said. "But the bakery two doors down left their feed on a public login after that delivery dispute."

"Pull it," I said.

He did. A grainy view of bins and a sliver of asphalt popped up. At 18:09:18 two figures edged into the corner of the frame. White jacket, gold flash, blue tote. They stopped near the gate while Daria typed. Marin kept her phone still, face tipped toward the tree line of the lot beyond. At 18:09:32 Daria looked down the alley toward the street and then raised her phone high as if searching for a signal. At 18:09:36 the feed glitched. When it returned at 18:09:41 the corner was empty.

"Blind spot between bins," Rafi said.

"Seen it," I said. "We have their approach. We have the time."

I pulled Seth's earlier file to the stand and tapped the info pane. Creation time stamped 18:20. Ten minutes before the club hour printed on the invite. Ten to the dot.

"Align it," I said.

Rafi lifted a card. "Meet at eighteen oh eight thirty. Vanish into the lot at nine forty-one. Seth's spine photo at twenty," he said. "Our two walk past the camera toward the lot just as he shoots a book that struts in oranges and rings. That gives ten minutes to handle a case, stage a pass, or whatever show they sold each other."

"And that paints our timeline without drama," I said. "Daria meets Marin at our door and walks her toward the side lot nine minutes before Seth's 'yesterday' photo."

Miss Dotty wrote it in the ledger beside a neat margin number and underlined the words without pressure.

"City cameras," I said. "We need the council route feed on the snick between here and the lot."

"Already pinged," Rafi said. "Havel's tech sent a temporary code. Two cams on the snick. One at the back of Paula's Flowers, one by the pay meter."

He split the screen. Paula's Flowers gave us a slanted view of legs and elbows at knee height. At 18:09:20 a pair of ankles and one blue canvas corner jogged past. At the pay meter, a softer angle, we caught two backs for a half second, then the frame winked with a passing van's headlamp. When the light cleared, the backs had turned into a white smear of jacket and the blue corner of a tote slipping right.

"Print them," I said. "Throw away the ones that look like clouds. Keep the ones that court will accept."

Rafi printed four. We bagged two. We dated and signed across the tape as if the city would test us on neatness later.

My phone buzzed. Asa. He did not waste his syllables.

"Timed the meet," he said. "I see the upload. Good."

"We have Daria with Marin at our door at eight past," I said. "They walk to the lot. Ten minutes later Seth shoots his spine."

"We will weave them back to back," he said. "The board stands straighter when times do not wobble."

"Any joy on the club phones," I said.

"Enough," he said. "Havel got me a preliminary dump of the club's main host line and the director numbers for yesterday. No content. Only handshakes."

"Between whom," I said.

"Lin to Mott, eleven oh three and sixteen seventeen," he said. "Short strings. He responded to both."

"Thank you," I said.

"Do not swing it like a hammer," he said. "People mistake volume for guilt. We stack, we do not shout."

I smiled at the screen. "Stack, not shout," I said. "Yes."

He hung up. Rafi had already printed the handshake summary from Asa's secure share. Two lines, time, originating number, destination, duration. Sparse as a monk's lunch. Enough to plant a seed.

"Daria to Walter at eleven and sixteen," I said. "Two taps under six minutes total."

"Topic," Rafi said.

"We will ask both," I said.

Miss Dotty underlined the times and added a small note at the edge of the ledger. She writes in a hand that jurors can read from three chairs away.

I called Havel. He answered on the first ring.

"Got your stills," he said. "Good line. I have Marin for ten words. She remembers a bright jacket and the phrase quick peek. Then the trunk goes dark."

"Marin's a seller," I said. "She hears money when a room murmurs."

"She will hate herself for that sentence later," he said, still kind.

"Council feed gives us their backs," I said. "Enough to fix route and time. Asa has Lin to Mott at eleven and sixteen. No content. He will not wave it like a banner. He wants it in the file so the ink and dots have company."

"Good," Havel said. "I am en route to Walter. He answered on the second ring and sounded helpful enough to sell me a vacuum."

"Rafi and I will meet you there," I said. "Ten minutes."

"Watch your shoes," he said, then hung up.

Rafi killed the feeds. We sealed the sleeves. I wrote a single card for the board. Meet at the cat, eighteen oh eight thirty, walk to lot, Seth spine at eighteen twenty. Lin texted Mott eleven and sixteen.

Miss Dotty slid a small envelope across the table with two crisp tens and a coffee card. "Gina likes sweet," she said. "She lives two doors down from Walter. Make her a friend."

"We know how to live," Rafi said.

Peppermint stretched, flicked his tail at the door, and returned to the chair like a king who trusts his guard. We left the back light on. We lock cameras out of habit. Our alley never stops watching.

The garage sits behind a row of houses near the canal, green door, gravel break, oil stains that look like a Rorschach for men with socket sets. Havel's car was already there. He stood with a uniform at the edge of the drive and ate the last of a mints tin like it was dinner.

"Coffee for Gina as requested," I said, holding up the bag. "Two pastries, no raisins."

He nodded toward the left. "Her door is the one with the horseshoe," he said. "She stepped out when my uniform knocked on Walter's. She wanted to know whether this was about noise or fire. I said neither. She said thank you. You will like her."

Walter opened the green door before we reached it. He wore a flannel shirt with the sleeves rolled and a grin he likely put on in the mirror. The bench behind him carried three knives, two dull, one too eager. A long cardboard cradle sat at an angle on a table heavy with old catalogs. A heater buzzed under a shelf.

"Friends," he said to the air. "The cavalry rides. Come in. Forgive the mess."

"We will stand," Havel said, mild and even.

Walter spread his hands. "Suit yourselves. I have nothing to hide."

I looked past his shoulder and clocked the table dents, the dark rings from coffee, the old cover boards stacked near a rag bin, and the new blade in its sleeve. Rafi stepped to the side and scanned the floor for fibers someone might call stray.

"Walter," I said. "Yesterday at eleven and sixteen you and Daria exchanged texts."

He blinked once. "Fonts," he said. "She wanted an opinion on a club flyer. You know how she is. Fancy now, not legible. I told her to pick a face that loves readers."

Havel watched his mouth and not his hands. "Which face," he said.

"Caslon," Walter said without hesitation. "Always a winner."

"For a flyer about firsts," I said. "Caslon in a room that throws neon off gold."

"It sells taste," he said. "It whispers history."

He said the word I do not use when paper hangs between two teeth. I did not correct him.

"Give me your phone," Havel said.

Walter handed it over with a little flourish, one palm held up as if to show he hid nothing. Havel tapped with care and then handed it to the uniform. The uniform bagged it and signed a line on his clipboard.

"Club phone too," Havel said. "We will follow up with counsel."

Walter's grin thinned. "Counsel," he said. "We are friends."

"We are careful," Havel said.

Walter pivoted to the bench as if to avoid looking at the bag. He rested his hand on a metal straightedge with pin points along the edge. His thumb grazed a nick in the table where a knife had lived a bad day. The heater clicked.

"Did you see Daria yesterday in person," I said.

"Of course," he said. "She lives at the club. Everyone sees her if they breathe near that bar."

"Here," I said. "Not there."

He smiled at the floor. "She swung by last week for a poster roll," he said. "Not yesterday."

"Marin met her at our door at dusk," I said. "They walked toward the side lot. The time rubs up against a spine photo Seth took at eighteen twenty."

Walter watched my mouth now. He scratched his jaw. He left a small smear of something beige on his skin where his hand had picked up dust from the bench. Rafi watched the smear. I watched his eyes find the heater and stay there as if warmth would write him a story.

"Wild," he said. "I was here at that hour."

"Alone," Havel said.

"Gina two doors down can vouch for noise," Walter said. "She hates it. I gave her laugh tracks in exchange for her tolerance once."

"Coffee for her," I said, lifting the bag.

"Smart," he said.

Havel nodded at the table. "What were you cutting," he said.

"Boards," Walter said. "Old ones. A friend needs a cradle for a tired binding. I told them the truth about their wallet. They cried, then they paid."

"The friend's name," I said.

"You know I do not kiss and tell," he said, warm again.

"Fonts," I said. "Back to that. What did she ask you at eleven."

He leaned on the bench as if his back hurt. "She wanted a headline to pop without looking like a nightclub," he said. "I pushed her toward taste."

"And at sixteen," I said.

"Same," he said. "She panics twice before dinner."

Rafi cleared his throat. He took a folded print from his pocket and set it on the corner of the bench. Two lines. Eleven oh three. Sixteen seventeen. Lin to Mott. Duration numbers that did not match panic calls. Short, yes, but wrong rhythm for fonts. Sixteen seconds. Twenty-two seconds.

"Fonts in sixteen seconds," I said. "Twice."

Walter kept the smile. It slid at the edges now. "Her attention span," he said. "You know how she skims. She sends a link. I skim. I send a yes. We are modern."

"Send the links," Havel said. "We will look."

"I will when my phone returns from its spa," Walter said.

"Stop," Havel said. "You are not funny."

Walter swallowed.

"Did she ask you to meet her near the lot," I said. "Did she ask for help moving a case. Did she ask about grid dots on spines."

"Fonts," he said. "We talked about fonts."

"Which subface of Caslon," I said.

He tried to say it lightly and failed. "Old Style," he said. "You know. The classic one."

"You mean the umbrella," I said. "You did not talk about fonts."

His eyes flicked to the door. Havel did not turn to follow the look. He did not need to.

Gina opened her door anyway, drawn by gravity and coffee. She looked at the four of us and the heater as if she had seen this exact play too many times. I handed her the bag. She opened it, pulled a pastry free, and took a bite without blinking.

"He says fonts when he lies," she said around a crumb. "Last month it was kerning."

Walter flushed. The heater clicked again. The knives on the bench stayed where they were, quiet and sharp.

I took one step toward the cradle. He stepped between me and the table in a way that made his helpful smile look thin.

"We do not lift," I said. "Not without paper. We came to fix the meet. We did."

Havel slid the bagged phone into his case and wrote a time on his pad. "We will see you again tonight," he said to Walter. "Do not leave."

"I host," Walter said. "I do not hide."

"We will test that sentence," Havel said.

We walked out into the cold without a good-bye. The canal smelled like mud and old rope. A gull argued with a bin lid and lost.

Rafi blew into his hands and looked at me. "He grabbed 'fonts' like a float," he said.

"He is lying," I said.

CHAPTER 15

Footage Frame

By two ten the board behind the counter looked like a clean argument learning to walk. Dot grid on the left. UV strip in the middle. Alley stills on the right. Under it, a card that read in Miss Dotty's hand: Marin alive. Books bait. Trunk lip says warm sand.

Havel called from the curb. I left the bell to Peppermint and met him at the door.

"Title Office sits across from the south wing," he said. "Their cameras do what the hospital's do not. Stairwell and corner lot. Guard likes forms. Bring your chain."

We cut through the drizzle and reached a lobby made of linoleum and patient carpets. The Title Office security room lived in a glass cube by the staircase, with a fan that tried and a monitor wall that did more than try. A guard in a navy cardigan set down a sandwich and stood when he saw Jude. His badge read K. Osei. His eyes read awake.

"DI," he said. "We made pulls by time stamp. I printed logs to keep the line clean."

"Thank you, Mr. Osei," Havel said. "This is Ms. Wren."

Osei nodded, then pointed to a chair I would not use. "You will want Stairwell 3, cam two, and Exterior South, cam one," he said.

"Stairwell gives you a shoulder view with detail. Exterior gives you the lane between the trees and the row. Hospital cam two watches the trunk. All set to the same clock after the loop hiccup last month."

"Roll Stairwell 3," I said.

He did. At 13:27 the stairwell showed a pair of shoes and a white jacket sleeve breaking the frame. Camera angle sat high. The wearer kept to the wall. No face. The shoulder carried a canvas tote with enamel pinned along the lip like medals. I counted four. A crown with five points. A round slice of citrus. A block letter in black. A tiny cat head with blue eyes. The tote strap rode the left shoulder. The pins faced forward.

"Stop at thirteen twenty-eight twenty," I said.

He froze. The frame caught the tote in hard light at the turn. The crown pin had a nick at the second point, a chip where metal meets enamel. The citrus slice glowed fake and bright. The cat eyes gave the lens judgment. The letter pin sat as a lone black square with a serif D in white.

"Print three," Havel said.

Osei printed without asking for paper. He slid the sheets to me. I dated the top margin, wrote the cam label and time, and signed the edge. Havel countersigned. Osei wrote a pull log in neat block letters and handed it across.

"Exterior South next," I said.

He keyed it up. At 13:31:44 the lane came alive. Nurses crossed, a volunteer wheeled a stack of clipboards, a delivery van blocked the far blind. Our frame watched the edge of Marin's row. Her hatchback sat two cars in from the end, back toward the camera. At 13:32:07 the white jacket sleeve entered from the Title Office door frame and crossed toward the row. The tote rode high. The pins flashed once in the sun like small eyes. The strap slid a notch. The wearer adjusted with a small shake without breaking stride.

"Closer," I said.

Osei zoomed the stored feed. The image softened but held enough shape to hurt. The tote brushed the rear quarter panel of a car as the wearer squeezed past, landed near Marin's rear door, then slid out of frame toward the trunk line. The camera did not give a face, but it gave size and movement. Chin high. Step light. Phone in the right hand. Same as yesterday at the alley. Same as the club.

"Time," Miss Dotty would say. I read it out loud even though she was three blocks away.

"Thirteen thirty-two twenty-one," I said. "Trunk shut at one forty-eight. Figure at the lip at one thirty-three. We have our tote at thirty-two."

Osei tapped the keyboard and split the screen to show Hospital cam two in the corner. We watched the figure press the lip. We watched the wipe. Then we watched them leave the frame like a guilty breeze.

"Print those two on one page," Havel said. "Without faces. With the clock."

Osei printed. I wrote a clean caption in ink along the edge. Stairwell 3, cam 2: white jacket, tote with crown, citrus, letter D, cat. Thirteen twenty-eight twenty. Exterior South, cam 1: tote brushes quarter panel by Marin's row. Thirteen thirty-two twenty-one. Hospital cam 2: trunk press and wipe. Thirteen thirty-three even.

"Back to Stairwell 3," I said. "Reverse four minutes. I want the entry."

He scrubbed backward. At 13:24 the stairwell showed empty steps and a stenciled sign about patience. At 13:25:02 the white sleeve and tote entered from the top, moved down, paused at the landing, then continued. The wearer kept to the right. The tote rode against the rail and knocked a small enamel tap off the metal.

I saw it happen in the frame. A tiny bounce at the lip. A pin dropping in a small arc, catching the stair edge, rolling to the base where the riser meets the tile.

"Freeze," I said.

The pin glinted once on the tile edge before the camera auto-adjusted and lost it in the floor pattern.

"Print that," Havel said. "Then we will fetch it."

Osei printed. He lifted the phone and called the stairwell porter. A woman in green pants showed up with a broom and the face of a person who cleans real things while everyone else talks. We met her at the landing with a small flashlight and a soft brush.

"Picture says corner of the first riser," I said. "Meet point with the wall."

She kneeled and swept with grace. The brush caught something that clinked once against metal. She glanced up and then passed it to me on the tip of the bristles.

An enamel crown, five points, second point nicked. Bent post. No back. Dust along the edge. Warm sand in a faint smear along the lower corner where it had kissed the floor during a wipe.

I did not say the color out loud. I did not need to.

I slid the crown onto a clean card and photographed it with today's paper in the frame. I signed the card and wrote the time and the place. Havel read the line to Osei and Osei wrote it into the log. The porter watched and did not ask for a show. She had seen enough shows in life to hate them.

"Bag," Havel said.

I dropped the crown into a small pouch, added the card, sealed, signed across the tape, and handed it to him. He signed under mine, then slid the bag into a larger envelope labeled Title Office Stairwell, 13:25 pin recovery.

"Exterior sweep," I said.

We left the cube and walked out to the row. A trap of drips collected near the trunk line from the last storm. Rafi arrived with gloves in his pocket and patience in his hands. Osei stepped out with a magnet on a string and a small bench brush. We looked like a group who had lost a button in a laundrette and cared too much.

"Under the car," Rafi said, kneeling by Marin's right rear wheel. He aimed the light along the lip and tilted his head. "I have metal," he said. "Not a screw. Not a nut."

He slid the magnet under the car and skimmed the lip. The crown did not care about magnets. Enamel wins that fight. What the magnet did grab was a back clasp in gold, the kind that pin makers sell in bags by the hundred.

"Photo," I said.

Rafi held steady while I framed the clasp with today's paper and a scale card. Osei wrote the time. Havel bagged the clasp in a second pouch and signed the seam. Rafi went back under and swept. The brush collected gravel and dust and a second treasure. A tiny circle, bright orange with a slice pattern, paper scrap glued to the back where a pin's clasp would seat. Citrus slice enamel pin, face down, chip on one wedge.

"Two for one," he said, and did not smile.

We repeated the photo and the bag. Now we had a crown from the stairwell and a citrus slice from under the car. Two pins from the same tote, one at the landing, one at the row. Two times that hugged the trunk frame.

The board in my head clicked a tooth. I called Asa.

"Stairwell caught the tote at thirteen twenty-eight with crown, citrus, letter D, cat. Exterior shows tote near Marin's row at thirty-two. Hospital shows trunk press and wipe at thirty-three. We pulled a crown pin in the stairwell. We pulled a citrus pin under the car. Clasp near the lip. Warm sand on crown edge."

He exhaled once. "Add to file," he said. "Write in five words for a judge."

"Pins match tote near trunk," I said.

"Good," he said. "Leave adjectives at home. Send stills now. Bring pouches at four."

We walked the time line again, this time in ink on my pad while Osei printed a log for the exterior pull. Jude had the guard sign in three places. He likes signatures stacked like a small fence.

"Next piece," Havel said. "Title Office had a visitor at noon with the same tote, but the pins sat in a different order. Do we care."

"We care," I said. "People move pins without thinking. They fall. They re-pin. But the crown nick will match to the one in the feed."

Osei pulled the noon clip. Same tote. Same pins. The crown nick read clean. The citrus chip read clean. Pin order differed by one slot on the lip. The letter D sat on the far edge rather than middle. She had adjusted between noon and one. That made sense for someone who fussed in mirrors.

Rafi printed stills and we filed them. Miss Dotty would want the noon frame beside the one at twenty-eight. She loves pairs.

In the guard room the clock ticked toward three. Havel tucked the pouches into his case and looked at me. "Do you want the talk or shall I," he said.

"We both do," I said. "You ask on record. I follow with the line she thinks she can step across."

He called the number and set his phone to speaker. Daria answered with a cheerfulness I have heard from waiters right before a sink floods.

"Detective," she said. "I was about to ring you. Our reveal wants a new time. Sponsors ask, I try to keep them happy."

"Stop trying," he said. "We need you in the Title Office lobby in ten. Bring your tote."

"My tote," she said. "How cute."

"Bring it," he said. "Bring all the little pins."

"Pins fall off all the time," she said, ready with an alibi before the question. "If you found one, I will buy you a fresh set for your desk."

Havel hung up without a good-bye. He stared at the phone for a count of three and then put it in his pocket like a pen. He does not waste anger.

"Lobby," he said.

We stood under a soggy poster about land records and waited. Daria arrived in white, fresh concealer along the thumb line I knew too well, tote on the left shoulder. The lip held three pins and a gap. Crown missing. Citrus missing. Letter D and cat still clung. The strap showed a new bend where a person had fidgeted in a stairwell.

"Here I am," she said. "Smile for a tedious camera."

Havel did not. "Where are your pins," he said.

"They fall off all the time," she said. "Sure."

CHAPTER 16

Printer Admits

Walter left the green door wide and stepped back from the bench. No heater hum. No music. Oil smell and paper dust sat quiet on concrete.

Havel stood in the mouth of the door with his notebook low. Rafi set the field kit by the sawhorse and kept his hands in his pockets. I placed my folder on the table and laid out the order like a clean meal.

"Dot grid," I said, setting Len's signed sample sheet photo on the left and our spine photo on the right. "House grid here. Your dot rides high by a mill here. Consistent on the sheet you ran and the sheet in my case."

Walter's eyes stuck to the left photo for two breaths, then slid to the right, then lifted to my face. The grin he wore for most of a life took one step back.

"Acid nib," I said, placing the small steel holder from his pegboard in the center. "Pen point loaded with weak acid for fast halos, used on donor sheets to make sponsors clap at dinner."

He did not deny the tool. He reached to straighten it, stopped, and put both hands flat on the edge.

"Side cash," I said, laying down three notes from Len's ledger, the week ticks where Walter's column runs heavy, and a printout of two bank withdrawals made near midnight in the months we flagged. "You call it helping friends. The work lived here."

He looked at Havel as if the detective might rescue him from me. Havel said nothing. His face gave him no door.

"Speak plain," I said. "I brought the grid to set the year. I brought the nib to set the type of lie. I brought your side jobs to set intent."

Walter's shoulders loosened. The fight drained as if the floor had a valve.

He pulled a rag from his pocket, folded it into a careful square, and set it under his right palm like a small stage block. He leaned on it and kept his voice level.

"I built a colophon sheet," he said. "Donor paper. Real donor stock from a box that should never have left a cold room. Money on the barrel. I set type to ape the year and faked the pin marks with a plate I made from a scan. My dot grid missed by a mill because I worked off a second hand frame and lied to myself about the risk."

Rafi did not move. Havel wrote one word, then waited.

Walter looked at the steel nib on the table like it had a name. "I warmed the edge for the look sponsors love," he said. "Not with a bath. With that nib and a slow line, less harm, more brag. Stupid, but it sells. I told myself it was a dress, not a body."

"Where did it land," I said.

He tapped the right photo where the high dot sits by the fold. "Inside a copy that walked through a club. I sold the sheet alone. A buyer laid it in a book. I did not lift a leaf or touch a paste-down. I told myself the sin ended at my door."

"Your buyer yesterday," Havel said.

Walter shook his head. "I did not meet the seller in the lot. I did not touch her car. I stayed here, made coffee taste like cardboard, tried not to read my phone."

"Name the buyer," Havel said.

Walter looked past us toward the canal as if the water would answer for him. It did not.

"Name the buyer," I said, softer than Havel, but closer.

"Daria," he said. "She came with cash. She wanted a colophon on donor stock to dress a copy for a reveal. No receipt. No club letter. No paper trail. I told her no three times. The fourth time I liked the shape of the number and I liked the way she said first as if it blessed the room."

"How much," Havel said.

Walter rubbed the folded rag with his thumb. "Enough to make a week feel easy," he said. "Not enough to fix a year."

"Show me the leftover," I said.

He did not ask how I knew he still had some. Men like Walter keep one more piece than they should, a hedge against a doorbell. He walked to a tin under the bench, opened it without theatre, and lifted two boards, three sleeves, and a brown wrap that smelled like a bar. He sorted without hurry and brought one sleeve to the table.

"Here," he said.

Inside lay a donor sheet with the same cream tone we saw in the old press room, but with a throat that looked wrong to anyone who has measured this house. The dot at the lower left rode high. The kiss of the plate sat soft. The edge wore a narrow ring of brown that glowed strange in our light.

"UV," I said.

Rafi flicked the lamp. The ring blinked to life, coral and wrong. Walter did not watch the glow. He stared at the dot, that tiny mill of guilt.

I set Len's photo beside the sheet and used the pressman's old straightedge with pin points to show the line. The points landed true on the sample, then missed by a hair on Walter's sheet. I marked the miss on a sleeve card with a pencil. No flourish. No lecture.

"I failed the grid," Walter said, before I spoke. "I told myself nobody would see it because nobody teaches dots to donors. Then I remembered you read dots." He smiled without joy. "You and your cat and your little chain cards."

"You call this a fake colophon," Havel said. "Say it."

"A fake colophon sheet," Walter said, each word slight and honest. "Printed off a scan. Laid on donor stock. Trimmed shy to slide in neat. Haloed for room applause. Sold for cash."

"To Daria Lin," Havel said.

"To Daria," Walter said. "Alone, at my table, door open. She told me it would sit in a frame. She told me it would never ride in a book where truth matters. She knew where a lie buys attention and where it buys cuffs."

"Dates," I said.

He swallowed. "First meet three weeks back. First cash a day later. Pickup two days before your seller's trunk."

"Yesterday," Havel said.

"I did not see her," he said. "She did not text for a sheet. She texted for fonts to give us cover if someone ever pulled phones."

"Origin of her phrase good one," I said. "Does she use it in your texts."

"Every third line," he said. "Good one for a font. Good one for a tea. Good one for a time. She has a string for it. When she wants to sell a shortcut she calls it good."

I slid the donor sheet into a sleeve, photographed it with today's paper, and wrote the chain line while Havel read the time to me. Walter signed the sleeve without prompting. His hand shook and the scrawl went ugly. He stared at it as if ugliness were the real crime.

"Walk me through your plate," I said. "Briefly."

"Scan, clean, plate on a cheap bed," he said. "No cylinder. No kiss worth the name. I made marks to mimic pin holes because people who sell rooms think holes equal old. My grid missed because my bed lies on the left by a hair. I knew the lie. I chose speed and money."

"Where is the plate," Havel said.

"Cut," Walter said. "I do not keep faces in drawers."

"We will search anyway," Havel said.

Walter nodded. "You will not find a face," he said. "You will find a bed I should have burned and knives I should have dulled."

"Why tell me now," I said. "You had a lie ready in your mouth when we walked in. Fonts."

He looked at his bench. "The crown pin in the stairwell gave me a knot," he said. "Then the citrus under the car made the knot pull tight. I do side favors. I sell neatness. I do not stuff women in trunks. If I keep your work out of a trunk, I help. I am old enough to pick help."

He turned the rag again. The square had lost its shape.

"Daria paid in cash," Havel said. "What numbers."

Walter told him. Havel wrote them, slow and clean. "She came alone," Walter added. "Phones facedown. Jacket bright. Same gold at the throat. Sterile wipes in her bag. She cleans like a stage manager. I thought it was funny until I saw the way you wrote the trunk lip in your memo."

"You read our memo," I said.

"I asked Asa for the morning page when he leaned on me about your dot," Walter said. "He treats me like a boy who might have told the truth already. I do not hate him for it."

Rafi opened the trash with a foot pedal and set out a bag for any new piece. He has the same respect for neatness Len has. He never throws a thing at a bin, he always places it.

"Anything else on donor stock," I said.

Walter lifted the tin again and laid the contents bare. Two sheets with the off grid, one with a failed edge halo, one clean. He had written No in pencil across the clean one, then kept it anyway. He placed them where we could see and did not reach for any.

I bagged both and wrote the chain while Havel read the clock and signed. Rafi held the tape so I would not smudge the seam. Walter watched without a twitch.

"Tell me about Marin," Havel said.

"Seller," Walter said. "I know her face from markets and halls. She likes a list and a list likes her. I never met her here. I never sold to her. She does not buy my kind of sin."

"She answered a VIP text," I said.

He closed his eyes. "Of course she did," he said. "Daria writes a VIP text like a hymn."

"You had a knife out yesterday," Havel said, looking at the bench.

Walter pointed to the dull pair. "I flattened boards with those," he said. He touched the new one in its sleeve. "This one I had sharpened for clean cradle cuts this week. It is still in paper, you can take it."

Havel bagged the new blade and signed. He set it aside without comment. He does not let a clean line of evidence spoil because he has a clever day.

"Walk us to your back room," I said.

He did. Two steps and a pivot around a stack of old catalogues. The back held a rack with strips of board and a small light. On the wall, taped in the order of a man who craves control, sat a row of prints from club events where Walter's work rode in shadows. A poster with serif letters. A caption card with bad kerning. He could not hide the itch even when he lied. He always left a thread for a person like me to pull.

"Why her," I said, pointing to nothing and asking about Daria.

"She makes rooms feel safe until they are not," he said. "That sells."

"You wanted to stop," I said.

He looked at his thumbs, then at the floor. "After the first cash I thought yes, stop," he said. "Then the morning after I missed the weight of the envelope. And I liked the way she said first like a blessing."

He raised his face and saw how that sounded. He flinched and tried again. "I wanted to stop," he said. "I did not."

He took a breath that shook. "She will tell you I am small," he said. "She will be right. I am small the way a rat is small. I make fast runs in dark spaces and pretend I am saving a feast from air. I am not saving anything."

Havel let the silence sit. He knows when to let a man hear himself.

"Phone records," Havel said at last. "You said cover texts on fonts. Did you delete anything else."

"I do not scrub," Walter said. "I lack patience for that sort of purity."

"We will see," Havel said.

Rafi lifted the nib holder and nodded at me. I photographed it with today's paper, then set it back. We did not bag it. Tools live on benches in this city; a tool only earns a pouch when a name sits on the cut.

"Do you have a partner on these sheets," I said.

He shook his head. "My sin fits in one pair of hands," he said. "Len knew my taste for favors. He did not know I spread it to plates."

"You used the word plate with care," I said. "You did not brag about kiss or impression because you know your touch fails under a loupe."

"I know where my line lives," he said. "I stepped over it with a fake. I still know the words for what I failed to do."

The uniform at the door cleared his throat. Havel nodded without turning. The uniform went back to watching the neighbors.

"Daria wanted to stop too," Walter said, and laughed once with no joy. "She told me that after the first cash. She said, Walter, this scares me, we stop after tonight. Then she texted me two days later with a crown emoji for a pin and said your good one landed."

"Crown," I said.

He touched his collarbone where a pendant might sit. "She wore the pin set like a sash," he said. "Crown over citrus over cat. Letter D on the edge for ego. She told me pins fall off all the time. She said it like a prayer that forgives the floor."

"Pins fall off all the time," I repeated, taste of tin in my mouth.

He looked past us again. We let him. Outside, the canal muttered under a small wind that brought a hint of rain. The sound made the garage feel smaller and more honest.

"You will charge me for the sheets," Walter said to Havel. "Charge me for the tool if you find poison on it. Charge me for the lies. Do not tie me to the trunk. I stayed hungry and afraid in this room. I earned that, not the trunk."

"You are not in the trunk file," Havel said. "You are in my fake file. They walk together until one of them turns right."

Walter blinked and nodded. "Thank you for the sentence," he said.

Havel closed his notebook. "We are done for now," he said. "Stay reachable. Counsel will love you less than you think."

Walter half smiled. "Counsel loved me once," he said. "We did a gala with lanterns. I printed place cards with a pearl coat. They paid me in praise. It has not stuck."

I packed the photos and the bagged donor sheets. Rafi took a last sweep of the floor by the bench for any loose scrap that wanted to jump to a shoe. He placed two fibers in a pouch and wrote Floor by vice, near blade sleeve. He signs like a man who ran a mailroom before he ran a shop.

At the door I paused. "You keep the door open," I said.

He nodded. "I talk less when it shuts," he said. "That never helps."

We stepped into the damp. Gina stood under her horseshoe with a mug and a brow like a beam. I lifted the empty pastry bag. She lifted her mug in reply.

"He talk," she said.

"He confessed to his part," I said.

"Then he will sleep," she said. "First time since he touched that fool plate."

"We will come back," Havel said.

"I will still hate noise," she said.

We walked to the car. Rafi drove. I sent Asa the line he asked for weeks ago when he said this case would tip on simple words.

Walter admits fake colophon on donor stock. Off-grid dot matches our sheet. Acid nib used to halo. Never met seller yesterday. Buyer named: Daria Lin. Paid cash.

His reply landed before the first light turned green. Logged. See you at four. Bring the sheet and the plate story. Good clean page.

I looked out at the canal and did not reward myself with relief. We had a man who names a buyer. We had pins from a stairwell and a row. We had a trunk lip that wore makeup. We had a host who wants a reveal to launder a lie.

I still needed Marin's clear voice, and I still needed the face at the lip in a frame that even a sponsor would believe.

Rafi tapped the wheel twice. "Garage again tonight," he said.

"After the club," I said.

"Will she run," he said.

"She thinks rooms save her," I said. "She will not run until a room tells her to."

Havel called as we pulled into our street. "We served the club for phones," he said. "They whined. They will hand them over by six."

"And Daria," I said.

"She gave me a speech about building culture," he said. "Then she asked when she can host the reveal."

"What did you say," I asked.

"Never," he said.

The bell on our door chimed. Peppermint lifted his head as if we were late. Miss Dotty looked up from the ledger and read my face.

"He told the truth he owns," she said.

"He did," I said. "He named her. Paid in cash. He wanted to stop. He did not."

CHAPTER 17

Host Cracks

We take the back room. Four chairs. No stage. No bar light to flatter the wrong things. Miss Dotty sits with the ledger. Rafi runs the recorder. Asa takes center, jacket off, sleeves neat, pen capped.

Daria walks in with a tote on her left shoulder and a smile that asks the room to forgive her in advance. Two pins on the lip now, the cat and the D. The crown gap glares. The citrus gap glares more. Her right thumb wears fresh concealer. The nick hides, but not well.

"Asa," she says, sweet as peel. "If this is about optics, I can help."

"It is about facts," Asa says. "Sit."

She sits. She angles herself so the smile faces me and the eyes face him. She sets the tote on her feet as if we will pat it.

I pull the first card from the stack and lay it on the table.

"Eighteen oh eight thirty," I say. "Alley by my door. You and Marin meet here. You raise your phone. You turn your head to the side lot. You expect her to follow. She follows."

Rafi slides the still toward her. Alley frame. Her white jacket. The gold flash at her throat. Marin's blue tote. The sign above the back door reads Peppermint Cat. Time stamp sits clean in the corner.

"Cute," she says. "Neighbors meeting in a cozy alley. Put it on a postcard."

Second card.

"Eighteen twenty," I say. "Seth's spine photo. Deeper stamp, lower seat, oranges in the corner, ring on the right hand. Metadata set ten minutes before the posted hour."

Asa turns the print to face her. He taps the time in the info pane.

"You love rooms," I say to her. "Rooms love clocks. The wrong clock hangs you here."

She rolls her eyes small, a tic she uses when a room starts to slide away.

Third card.

"Twenty-one hours later," I say. "Title Office, Stairwell 3. Thirteen twenty-eight twenty. Your tote passes the camera. Four enamel pins on the lip. Crown with a nick at the second point. Citrus slice. Cat head. A block D."

Rafi pushes the still across the felt. The tote fills the frame. The crown nick catches the light. The citrus glows like a sign.

"Exterior, cam one," I say. "Thirteen thirty-two twenty-one. Same tote, same pins, brushing the lane near Marin's row. Hospital cam two at thirteen thirty-three. A hand presses her trunk lip. Same white sleeve in play. The thumb wipes the edge with tissue. The lip holds a smear the color of your concealer. We lifted it."

She glances at her thumb. She does not look down. The eyes go cold, the mouth keeps the smile.

"Pins fall off all the time," she says. "I walk in the world. It grabs."

I set the pouches on the table. Crown from the stairwell. Citrus from under the car. Clasp by the lip. Bags signed, dated. Today's paper in each photo.

"World your tote grabbed," I say. "Twice, when it mattered."

Asa does not speak. He stacks the bags to his right, tidy, patient.

Fourth card.

"Our ink test," I say. "UV strip, band climb. Rhodamine glow. Gel binder. Modern dye set not present at print date. Your margin quotes are a new hand."

Rafi places the photos where she can see the coral end of the dye trail. The masthead in frame reads the date. She watches my mouth, not the strip. People in her trade do not look at tools unless they play a part.

Fifth card.

"Dot grid," I say. "House sample from the year. Clean. Dot sits here. Your colophon sheet sits high by a mill. Walter's leftover carries the same miss."

Asa goes slow. He puts down Len's signed photo. He puts down the leftover from the tin. He sets the old straightedge with pin points between them and anchors the line. He says nothing. He does not need to.

Her face shifts a click. Not guilt. Arithmetic. She is counting where the room turns.

Sixth card.

"Phone," I say. "Club area code, noon yesterday. 'Bring the good one. Quick peek only. VIP needs it.' Marin's handset holds that invite."

"Club numbers love the word VIP," she says. "So do your readers."

"They love names," I say. "They will get yours."

Seventh card.

"Thumb," I say. "Your right one. Fresh peel. Fresh concealer. We watched you leave a dot of it in my shop at noon. We lifted two more from jackets you touched. The trunk lip wears the same tone, same slip."

"Makeup is not a crime," she says.

"Shoving is," I say.

She looks at Asa for an objection. He gives her a straight face and a capped pen.

Eighth card.

"Spine stamp," I say. "Seth's shot gives a deeper, lower bite than our glass copy. Either he shot a second copy, or someone did a piece swap. Your fake colophon sheet completes the set. You served a dressed book to the room last night, told them first, and hoped no one would check the bones."

Asa taps his thumb once on the table. Now.

"Walter says you bought a fake colophon for cash," he says. "He admits he set it. He says you told him it would sit in a frame. It did not."

Her eyes flash once. She hides it fast, but the spark hits the ledger.

"He is small," she says. "He likes hearing his name."

"So do you," I say.

I pull a fresh card and do the part I came to do, clean and straight.

"You staged a reveal with a dressed copy," I say. "You quoted modern margin lines like scripture. You clung to the word first. Marin sold you a real one and came to see where it would land. Somewhere between the meet and the ramp she saw the swap. She balked. You lost your temper and shoved her on the loading ramp, small, hard, the way a person moves a rolling rack out of a lane. No blood. Enough fear to ruin her night. Today you lured her to the hospital lot to scare her into silence. You pressed her trunk lip with a right hand and wiped your thumbprint with tissue. You did not plan for the crown pin to fall on the stair. You did not plan for our alley to hold time like a nail. Clout costs less than prison."

She stares at me. Then at the bags. Then at the strip. She tries to smile. It slips. Her tongue touches the place where people press when they want the next lie to arrive with poise.

"Marin pushed me first," she says. "She accused me of stealing. I do not steal. I host. I raised a hand to guide her past the ramp.

She leaned wrong. The room was tight. She stumbled."

"Words for your crowd," I say. "They do not survive here."

Asa folds his hands. "Was there a shove," he says.

Her mouth opens, shuts, opens. "A nudge," she says. "Fine. A nudge."

"Her shoulder or her back," I say.

"Shoulder," she says. "It was crowded."

"The cameras see the ramp," Rafi says. "You know this."

She blinks. One blink too slow.

"You will say the clip fails," I say. "You are used to blind spots."

"Pins fall off all the time," she says again, as if a phrase can be a life raft.

"Yours fell off where time holds," I say.

We sit with it. She looks at the tote. She looks at the gold at her throat. The room does not clap. Nothing saves her.

"Then write it your way," she says to me. "Write that I overreached. Write that I wanted the city to feel big again in a room I built. Write that I did not know where to stop."

"I will write where you pushed and where you wiped," I say. "That is enough for a spine."

She turns back to Asa. "What do you want," she says.

"Not want," he says. "What the file needs. We need you to confirm you bought a fake colophon, staged a reveal with it, and pushed Marin on the ramp when she balked. We need you to confirm you met her in our alley yesterday and walked her toward the lot. We need you to confirm you pressed the trunk and wiped your thumb. No adjectives. No stage."

Her jaw tightens. Her eyes go to the door as if someone will open it and bring applause.

"Do you have counsel," Asa says.

"I have contacts," she says.

"Call one when we are done," Asa says. "Right now we build the record."

"Record on what," she says, mocking the word and losing power.

Asa leans forward by an inch. He speaks like a stone. "On why the crown sits in a stairwell, why the citrus lives under a car, why your thumb color rides a trunk lip, why an alley shows you with the seller at eighteen oh eight thirty and a hospital feed holds your tote at thirteen thirty-two. On why a printer with knives says you paid cash for a lie. On why a donor sheet in your hand carries a dot that misses house practice by one mill."

Her head drops the length of a breath. She nods once. "He called me," she says, picking an easier lie. "He wanted to help. He said he could give me a way to keep the room from going flat. I said no. Then I said yes."

"Name him," Asa says.

"Walter," she says. "He is weak. He is useful. I am worse."

"Say the thing," I say. "Say you bought the sheet."

"I bought the sheet," she says, voice low, shame and pride wrestling. "In cash. From Walter. He called it dressing. I raised the money from a sponsor with a phone game and told myself it was a loan. I wanted the reveal. I wanted first. I always want first."

"Say the thing about the ramp," Asa says.

She does not speak for a hard ten seconds. Pigeons argue on the roof. The kettle in the front gives a polite sigh. Miss Dotty writes one clean line and waits.

"I told Marin her book would be part of a night the city needed," she says. "I told her the margins sang. She reads paper better than I thought. She saw the colophon sit wrong in the light when we turned the case. She grabbed my wrist. I shook her off. She stepped wrong. My hand was on her shoulder. She landed on the ramp edge. She cried. I panicked. I told everyone to make room. She left. I drank a drink I did not taste."

"Today," Asa says.

"I sent a text," she says. "VIP talk. Yes. I thought if I made it small, she would stop making it large. Show the good one and I give you something back. I said cash on return. I meant it. I walked her to the car and tried to talk sense into her at the trunk. I pressed the lip when she fussed with a wrap. I wiped the edge because that is what I do when I see a smudge. I did not put her in the trunk. I did not tie her hands. I did not gag her. I walked away."

"Your figure at one thirty-three," Rafi says.

"I walked away," she says again. "She sat angry in the driver's seat. I told myself she would drive. She did not."

"You will swear to that," Asa says.

"I will," she says.

He watches her. Watches her hands. Watches the throat. "We will test it," he says.

She nods. She points at the crown bag.

"I lost that on the stairs," she says. "I noticed after the Title Office. I told myself pins fall off all the time and bought a coffee."

"You did not think the crown would matter," I say.

"I thought the room would move faster than a pin," she says. "I was wrong."

"Say the margins," Asa says.

She shuts her eyes, opens them, and earns her first truth clean.

"The margins are modern," she says. "They are gel trash made by a person who wanted attention. I liked how they sounded in my mouth. I still do. I am not proud of that."

"You will give Jude your phone," Asa says. "You will list every number you used to invite Marin. You will write a statement that admits what we have and does not step on what we do not. You will not pick at the record with the kind of lies you sell sponsors for sport."

She takes a breath and reaches for her tote. Asa says no with a hand. She freezes. He pulls the tote from her feet and sets it on the floor by his chair. He looks at the pins. He looks at the gaps.

He does not smirk.

"I want a deal," she says. "I can give you names. Sponsors who paid for other lies. Managers who shift capacity. Club tricks. Museum staff who winked at favors. I can give you the shape of how rooms decide what is true. Let me walk in two years. Let me keep my house."

"Later," Asa says. "This is not where deals live."

"You will let Jude know I asked," she says.

"Jude will hear it," Asa says. "He will not clap."

She turns to me like a person still shopping. "You could write this kinder," she says. "You know how fear bends people. You have been bent."

"I will write clean," I say. "Kind makes the wrong parts breed."

Her eyes shift to the case light. She tries to fetch a reflection and cannot. She looks smaller now, same height, small anyway. She does not hide it.

"You like the word first," I say. "Keep it for the note you write to Marin. First to overreach. First to push. First to walk away from a woman in trouble."

"That is ugly," she says.

"That is on purpose," I say.

She presses her palms on her knees and keeps them there so we see that they are empty.

"What happens," she says to Asa.

"You do not leave town," he says. "You bring your phone to Havel by six. You keep your mouth shut around sponsors. You keep your hands off events. If I hear a hint of a reveal, I will bring an inspector with a click counter to your door."

She nods once. She stands. She does not reach for the tote. She looks at the ledger and reads the strip of Miss Dotty's neat lines.

"You write the way I wish I ran a room," she says to her. "It stays straight."

Miss Dotty lifts her gaze. "Rooms do not care what we wish," she says.

Daria walks to the door. For the first time since she stepped onto my floor, she looks at me without a pitch in her face.

"Tell Marin I am sorry," she says. "She will not believe me. Say it anyway."

"I will say it when she asks if you said it," I say.

She leaves. The bell does not cheer. The back room sags for a breath and then rights itself.

Rafi exhales. "She is not done lying," he says.

"She is done pretending the room saves her," I say.

Asa caps his pen and pockets it. "Good line," he says. "Use it if you like."

"Go give Jude the tape," Miss Dotty says. "And the tote if she tries to take it."

Asa nods. He lifts the bagged pins. He slides the leftover donor sheets into his case. He checks the time and writes a neat 15:07 beside it.

"Clout costs less than prison," he says, standing. "She understands that sentence. She does not understand about time."

"She will," I say.

He stops at the door and looks back at the table where the cards still sit in a clean row. "We froze her on the right things," he says. "Good work."

"Go feed Jude," Miss Dotty says. "We will mind the house."

When he is gone, the room shifts back. Rafi kills the recorder and labels the file. Miss Dotty adds one line to the ledger and closes it with the soft authority of a person who has closed worse.

I gather the cards and put them back in the box. Peppermint wanders in with a yawn and head-butts my ankle. He approves or wants a snack. Both ring true.

The phone buzzes. Havel: I have Marin again. She remembers the ramp. Shoulder. Shove. A phone line about VIP and good one. Bring me your pins at four.

Copy, I send. Statement coming. Host asked for a deal. Asa said later.

I lay a blank card on the mat and write the day's last line in ink so it cannot wobble. Staged reveal. Shove on ramp. Trunk at one thirty-three. Pins at thirteen twenty-eight and thirty-two. Ink modern. Grid off. Walter sold the lie. Daria paid in cash. Deal talk is for later.

CHAPTER 18

Recovery

Hospitals flatten sound. Footsteps land soft. Wheels murmur. Voices live in the throat and not the room. Rafi signed us in while I fed coins to the parking slip and pocketed the receipt like it might hold back bad luck.

DI Havel met us at the elevator with two coffees he did not drink. "She's awake enough to know her name," he said. "Doctor says short questions. We keep it clean."

We rode to the fourth floor. Afternoon light fell through a pane of glass that needed a better squeegee. I could see the south lot from the window near the nurse station. A white jacket cut across the row in my mind like a crease you cannot iron out. I let the image sit and walked past it.

Marin Grove lay propped on pillows that looked like clouds until you remembered the plastic covers. Oxygen cannula. Tape marks at her wrists where the EMTs had cut packing tape. A bruise rising under her hairline at the temple like a storm seeded by a careless hand. Her eyes held that stubborn light you see in sellers who count out change while someone tells them to hurry.

"Ms. Grove," Havel said, quiet. "I am DI Havel. This is Liora Wren and Rafi. We spoke near the car. You are safe. Take your time."

Marin breathed in as if her ribs had opinions. "I know you," she said to me. "Peppermint Cat. You taught a class on cloth spines and people who don't respect glue."

"I still teach it," I said. "Your tote met our alley camera."

"Good," she said. "Cameras like me when rooms don't."

Havel stayed at the foot of the bed. He opened his notebook but did not raise his pen. "We will ask four questions," he said. "You can stop us any time."

She nodded. I watched her watch the oxygen line. Sellers hate lines they did not set up themselves.

"First," Havel said. "Did you go to The Bindery to show a book to a host named Daria Lin."

"Yes," Marin said. "She pitched me with a word I do not love. VIP. I said the word buyer, she said the word moment. I walked anyway."

"Second," Havel said. "Did Ms. Lin push you on the club's loading ramp last night."

Marin closed her eyes. "Yes," she said. "Call it a shove. Her hand on my shoulder. I had two feet and then none. I caught the edge and sat down hard. She told me to relax. Then she put on a face for her people and the room swallowed it."

Rafi wrote one word on his card and left space. He writes like a carpenter cuts.

"Third," Havel said. "Did she lure you to the hospital lot today."

"Yes," Marin said. "Same voice. A story about family and relief. Bring the good one for a peek near the ward. Cash on return. I believed enough to regret it."

"Fourth," Havel said. "Did Ms. Lin place you in your trunk."

Marin opened her eyes all the way. Anger put color in her cheeks. "No," she said. "She did not tie my hands. She did not gag me. She pressed the trunk lip like a person who thinks cars obey. She wiped the edge like a person who cleans at parties. I sat in the driver's seat and called my cousin to complain. Then someone opened the trunk later, and the world took a nap I did not plan."

The nurse by the door lifted a finger. Havel nodded. "Two more," he said. "Short."

"Did you see Walter Mott yesterday," I asked.

"No," Marin said. "Not yesterday. I know his face from markets. He likes the sound of his name on a mic. That is all."

"Why bring the book to me first," I asked.

Marin let her mouth relax. "The club sells nights," she said. "Your shop sells truth. I wanted the first eyes to belong to someone who writes receipts before applause."

My throat did something I would not let it do here. I let the words land and said thank you in a voice that understood its job.

The nurse cut us off with a look that could herd cattle. "That's enough," she said. "She sleeps."

Havel closed his book. "We will come back when the doctor says so," he said to Marin. "You did well."

"Get the room that hurt me," she said. "I want to walk past it later without tasting copper."

"We will," he said.

We thanked the nurse and stepped into the hall. A cart rolled by with tea bags in a plastic bin and a stack of cups. Rafi stole two camomile packets with the grace of a saint. "For later," he said. "For Dotty's pocket jar."

We stood at the window by the elevator again and looked down at the south lot. The cars sat in neat rows pretending to be innocent. A gull hopped on a light pole and yelled for sport.

"Statement matches the cameras," Havel said, low. "She never saw Mott. She says the push. She says the text. She says the wipe."

"Her words hold," I said.

He looked at me as if I had asked for something. "You will get the book back on paper," he said. "Court and all that." He caught himself. "Court and the rest."

"I care about her shoulder," I said. "The paper will wait."

The elevator dinged like a polite bell. We rode down with a porter who smelled like antiseptic and cinnamon gum. He nodded at us as if he knew why knots in the city untied the way they did.

Outside, a sea breeze tried to clear the lot. It failed. We walked toward the curb. Asa's text pinged. Statement in progress. Pins logged. Bring the leftover donor sheets by four.

Copy, I sent.

Back at the shop, Miss Dotty already had the kettle on. Peppermint chirped from the sill like he wanted to file a report. Rafi hung his jacket and set the camomile in the jar. I stood at the board and wrote Marin confirms push on ramp. No Walter sighting. Book went to us first on purpose. I signed it and stepped back.

Talia came in halfway through a breath with her bag still on her shoulder. She looked smaller and older and newer all at once. The kind of day that burns layers you do not need.

"How is she," she asked.

"Alive," I said. "Clear enough to tell the part that matters."

Talia pressed her palms to the counter and held still. "Thank you," she said. "For not letting them make a narrative out of thin air."

"Thin air hates evidence," I said. "Today we fed it."

She blinked hard. Peppermint walked over and head-butted her hand with rude affection. She scratched his chin with fingers that had cleaned glass for three hours straight.

"Say the part you came to ask," Miss Dotty said from her stool. "It sits on your tongue."

Talia swallowed. "Tuition," she said. "Semester bills do not care about margins. If the book sells, I can finish the year. If this turns into a hold, I cannot. I do not want a sponsor to own my spine. I do not want the club to pitch a rescue and then send me a bill with parties on it."

Rafi leaned his hip against the table. "You have options," he said. "None taste like cake, but all feed you."

"We can float a shop loan," I said. "Paper and interest that make sense, not a trap. Work for us through spring, more hours on weekends, special events when we can stand it. We put it in ink. You keep your choices."

Talia exhaled like a person who does not like to ask and likes to be heard even less. "I can take more shifts," she said. "I can run the inventory backlog nights and list without missing. I can teach the intro class on boards. I can work for my help."

"You already do," Miss Dotty said. "This would honor that."

Rafi tapped the calendar pinned to the cork board. "There is also a bursary at the museum for students in book history," he said. "Silent application. Two letters. We can write one. Len Carter will sign the second if I bring him a biscuit."

"Len will do more than sign," I said. "He will teach you how dot grids sing to pressmen and how donors lie to themselves when watching plates kiss paper. You will like him."

Talia half smiled. "I like people who think ink is a verb," she said.

"Good," I said. "We will guide the bursary form tonight. We will walk a copy to the museum office before lunch tomorrow. You do not owe the club your future. You owe the work your attention."

Her eyes filled again and did not spill. "Thank you," she said.

"Another option," Rafi said, practical as a list. "We sell that run of midcentury jackets we saved for the spring fair. The shop takes the hit now. Receipts cover your tuition. We recoup when the copy war ends and our queue goes calm."

"Not a war," Miss Dotty said. "A correction."

"Fine," Rafi said. "A correction you can take to the bank."

Talia shook her head. "Do not torch your plan for me," she said. "I can stand on my feet. I do not want the shop to limp."

"You are the shop," I said. "We do this in pieces. Bursary if we can. Shop loan if we must. Class pay that respects the work. If the book sells clean, we rip up the paper. If it drags, you still study."

Talia gripped the counter harder. "I thought I could run with them," she said, meaning the club, the money, the rooms that clap. "Then I saw who they step on when they run."

"You saw it early enough to walk," I said. "Most people wait until the fall feels good."

She laughed once, raw and honest. "I do not like falling," she said.

"Me either," I said.

The bell chimed. A woman in a red coat asked for a mystery with trains. Rafi went to the stacks and returned with three titles and an extra smile. Miss Dotty poured tea, set one cup at my elbow and one at Talia's, and wrote a neat line in the ledger about the time and who sat in the back room to tell the truth.

I called Asa from the workroom while Talia found a tissue that did not disintegrate on contact with tears. "Marin confirms push," I said. "Confirms text, evening meet, wipe. Never saw Mott. Book came to us first by choice."

"Logged," he said. "Bring pins and donor sheets at four. Havel has phone pulls waiting. The club will try charm at six. I brought earplugs."

He hung up. He saves words for the part that pays.

I returned to the counter. Talia had found her center again. She folded the tissue into a cube and slid it into her bag like evidence of a person who fought and did not bleed out in public.

"Tell me what to do right now," she said.

"Eat," Miss Dotty said, handing her a biscuit from the jar. "Then write your bursary statement while the kettle hums. Start with the first book you held that told the truth about itself." She glanced at me. "Then Liora and I will write letters, and Rafi will print forms and make copies the way gods used to split seas."

"On it," Rafi said.

Talia bit the biscuit and nodded like a soldier with marching orders. Peppermint hopped back to the sill and glared at the pigeons and felt satisfied with his day.

I took the pins board off the wall, replaced it with a clean card for tonight's tasks, and looked at the line we had pulled into daylight. Marin would sleep. Daria would bring her phone to Havel because Asa had told her the names of the tools that visit when people refuse. Walter would sit in his open door and count his knives and he would not touch a plate.

Truth makes a spine. It holds a book upright. We had enough now to shelve this case on a row that made sense. Not done. Standing.

Talia finished her biscuit and squared her shoulders. "One more thing," she said. "When this sells, the first slice goes to Marin. She gets a cushion for the shove she took for our city's appetite."

"Yes," I said. "That is the only way to pay attention."

"You will write the note for the file," Miss Dotty said. "Names and numbers and how we send it. You will print it and sign. You will make good on it even if the club throws a parade."

"We will," I said.

The afternoon eased forward. Asa's four o'clock loomed. We packed the pouches and the leftover sheets and the straightedge Len had gifted us. Rafi lowered the case lights. Miss Dotty locked the till. Peppermint trotted to the door like a dog and then pretended he had not.

At the threshold Talia touched my sleeve. "Thank you," she said again, quiet. "For the book. For the spine. For the plan. For telling me where to stand."

"You did the standing," I said. "We gave you floor that holds."

She nodded and took her seat at the back table with a pen and paper and a face that wanted to be brave more than it wanted praise.

"Tuition," she said, half to herself, half to me. "We will solve it without a sponsor barging into my credits."

"We will," I said. "One honest line at a time."

CHAPTER 19

Restitution

The Title Office keeps a clean clock. Walls in municipal beige. Glass that shows you your own posture. Mr. Osei from Security waved us through with a nod and a clipboard. He did not offer commentary. He did not need to.

Conference Room B held a long table, four chairs on each side, a carafe of water, and a stack of forms no one loves. Asa set his case at the head and uncapped his pen. Miss Dotty opened the ledger and dated the page. Rafi plugged in the thin scanner we use when a room wants copies it can trust.

The estate lawyer arrived with a satchel and a careful face. Eda Farrow, gray suit with the patience to match. Marin came with her cousin and a sleeve on her wrist to keep the tape rash from picking a fight. Talia slipped into the seat beside me and kept her bag at her feet. She did not touch the carafe. She looked at the table as if it might ask her to run. It did not.

"Thank you for making the time," Farrow said. Voice level. No shine.

"We keep strange hours," Asa said. "Today they serve the truth."

We started with the binder. I slid it to the center, open to the first tab. Provenance line. Seller name. Photos from her aunt's boxes. The letter she wrote to herself the week her aunt moved the books from a city flat to a dry room upstate. Receipts from the last appraiser with stamps that line up with witnesses we can call. Then the page with the dot grid.

"Press foreman signed this," I said. "Year in question. House grid sits here. Our copy sits here too."

Farrow lifted the loupe Rafi brought and looked for herself. People who move paper for a living still like to see dots with their own eyes. She nodded once.

"Spine stamp," I said next. "Ours reads shallow and high. Consistent with Len Carter's sheet. The club feed's copy reads deeper, lower. We documented both."

Asa added the ink strip photos. UV shot. TLC bands. Rhodamine. Gel behavior. Date on the masthead in the frame.

"These refer to a dressed copy that stayed in the club," he said. "Not to this book. This book's margins are clean."

Farrow wrote a neat line in her notes. "Certified lab next week?" she asked.

"As needed," Asa said. "For now, this meets the office's threshold for a title record and a sale file."

Osei knocked and opened the door for DI Havel. He stepped in with two pouches and the same tired eyes that still catch small things. He placed the bagged donor sheets on the table and signed the intake line.

"From Mott's garage," he said. "Surrendered, as agreed."

Walter stood in the door's shadow, hat in hand in a way that did not help him. He kept his eyes on Eda Farrow, not on me. He had shaved. It did not change the shape of his week.

"You will read your statement," Asa said.

Walter read. Fake colophon on donor stock. Off-grid dot. Acid nib for a halo. Sold to Daria Lin for cash. No contact with Marin yesterday. He said each word as if it burned fraud taste off his tongue.

Farrow listened without blinking. When he finished she slid

a form toward him. "Voluntary surrender," she said. "And an administrative fine to the city's print heritage fund. Two figures. Painful but survivable."

Walter signed. He did not ask to bargain. He did not earn that right.

"Condition," Asa said. "No handling of donor stock for one year. No private jobs involving historical plates. If you touch a nib, it will be to write a card while somebody checks your ink."

Walter nodded. "Understood," he said. He set an envelope of cash on the table. Farrow counted without hiding it. She signed her line and slid a receipt across. He took the paper and did not look at it. He looked at Marin instead and said one sentence that did not beg.

"I am sorry," he said.

Marin took it and did not give him relief. She did not have any.

Seth came late. He came with a shirt designed to photograph well and a face that sells nights. He started to talk about timing and vibe before anyone asked a question. Havel raised a hand. "Stop," he said. "You will receive a written warning from Consumer Affairs for a misleading sales claim and a file note from my office about your post and the stall in your messages. If you post a correction, pin it. If you chirp, chirp about your correction."

Seth swallowed a sentence with sparkle on it and settled for a nod. "Fine," he said. "Pinned."

"Also," Asa said, "if you supply images to buyers going forward, you will supply the original file with full metadata when asked. You play rooms. You will not play courts."

Seth nodded again. The shirt did most of the performing for him. He made no eye contact with Marin. That, too, was a choice.

Farrow turned to the book. She asked us to lift it, show the colophon, count the gatherings, touch nothing we should not. The room held its breath while she read the key lines against the pressman's sample and her own notes. She checked the signatures we had logged on the chain cards. She checked the stamps on Len's sheet. She checked our initials on every tape. She wrote more notes. Then she closed her pad and looked up.

"The estate will sell the true first by sealed offer to a list that reads like a museum donor roster," she said. "Condition, read into this file: the book will reside in a public room. Access will not require a cocktail."

"Good," Marin said, from her seat in the corner.

"We also file a claim of injury against The Bindery for the shove and for the false margin story," Eda added. "That will find its own path. For title, we are done."

We all signed where the office needed names. Rafi scanned each page and labeled the files with codes that would make sense to a person who reads at three in the morning. Osei stamped the time on the master record. The clock did its job.

"One more piece," Farrow said. She took out a second folder with a red clip and placed it in front of Talia. "Your aunt's estate left a line in a will about education for the one who keeps the shop light honest. We could fight about which niece fits the sentence. Or we can do this. From the sale proceeds, ten percent will sit in a small fund earmarked for your current tuition and fees. Administered through my office. Without sponsor strings. We lodge it in this room now."

Talia looked at me, then at Miss Dotty, then at Eda. "You can do that," she said. Not a challenge. A check.

"I can," Eda said. "I did. The clerk will stamp this the same way he stamped your book."

Osei stamped. The sound was soft and satisfying, like a hinge that finally learns how to behave. Talia's face broke in a way that was not a cry. Relief has its own weight. She stood it.

Marin shifted in her chair and found a smile that fit her mouth. "Good," she said.

We signed the bursary lines. Miss Dotty wrote a clean note for our binder: Estate tuition carve-out, ten percent of net, Title

Office file number and today's date. Rafi took a photo of the filed form with the seal gleaming. Peppermint was not in the room. He did not need to be.

Asa packed the donor sheets, now city property. Havel gathered the pin pouches and the phone extracts. He would spend his evening with a screen and a frown. Seth slipped out with the speed of a man who saw no spotlight left. Walter left slower, without his swagger. He stopped in the hall and spoke to Gina on the phone in a voice a neighbor might forgive.

Eda gathered her satchel and shook our hands in that steady way good lawyers learn. "We put a book where it belongs," she said. "We pay a bruise with money and words. The rest will take what time it wants."

Outside, the sky held a pale sun. The river wind walked up the avenue and picked a few lids off bins, nothing dramatic. Rafi bought everyone street tea because the machine in the lobby drinks funds without loving you back. Marin's cousin drove her home to a block with fewer cameras and better soup.

Back in the shop, I wrote the Title Office docket number at the top of the board. Under it I wrote three lines for the day: True first filed with chain and lab. Donor sheet surrendered. Tuition fund set aside.

Talia looked at the card and then at me. "I still want the bursary," she said. "Not instead. With. I want the feeling of earning, not being rescued."

"You earned this," Miss Dotty said. "You leaned on the right wall. You did not sell the part of yourself that learns."

Rafi printed the bursary form and two sample essays from last year's winners so she could steal their structure and not their hearts. He loves a model. I love a line that knows where to end.

The phone rang. Eda again. "One more thing," she said. "We placed a call to the museum. They want to preview the book in your case room before the sale closes. Not a party. A visit. White gloves, clear table, three chairs, a clock."

"Fine," I said. "We prefer clocks to confetti."

She laughed once. "I thought so," she said. "We will see you tomorrow at ten."

I hung up and glanced at the cat. Peppermint blinked like a sage and went back to policing the pigeons.

I sent Asa a short note before he disappeared into his six o'clock: Title filed. Fine paid. Warning delivered. Tuition carve-out agreed. He wrote back one word. Logged.

The city unfurled into early evening. We turned the case lights low and left the board where it could be seen from the door. A regular came in for a mystery with a clock and a confession. I handed over two and kept one for myself for later. We earned one tonight.

Talia locked the till and tucked the filed copy of the tuition fund into a plastic sleeve that would not prove brittle in twenty years. She stood straighter. The day had not broken her spine. It strengthened it.

"Good," she said, as if answering a question the city had asked her since morning.

"Yes," I said. "Good."

CHAPTER 20

Final Words

C losing ran quiet. Lamps low. Case light at half. The kettle clicked once like a small clock that knew its job. Rafi counted the till. Miss Dotty drew a line across the ledger and capped her pen. The street thinned to bus hiss and the soft shoes of people who like the last train.

Peppermint chose the counter. He posted by the register with the self-importance of a tiny guard. Then he slid one paw into the slot where old receipts get lazy. A claw hooked something that did not belong with card slips and rubber bands. He dragged it out and patted it flat.

A torn slip. Cream stock, smooth, narrow blue rule. The edge showed a raw tear that matched the way a person pulls a page out of a glued pad. The ink wore that same steady line our seller used in her notebook yesterday at the nurse station when she wrote a phone number for her cousin. Loop on the g a touch theatrical. Crossbar on the t set low. Numbers neat, fives with flat tops.

I put on gloves. I slid a clean card under the slip and lifted both. Miss Dotty turned the ledger to a fresh line without being asked.

"Photo," she said.

Rafi set today's paper on the mat, masthead in frame. I took an overhead shot, then one at an angle to catch the tear fibers. The words sat on the page as if they had been waiting for the right light.

First hurt is mine. I met him when the presses ran nights and I let a story follow me home. D knows. She wants a room to eat it. Not this time.

It read like the tail of a note. Not a speech, not a post. Something a person writes in a pocket when they mean to tell a truth on their own terms. The hand matched Marin's. Not the gel foolery in the book. Her real hand. Ink dry. No tracer glow under UV. I checked anyway. Boring under the lamp in the way honest ink prefers.

"Where did it come from," Rafi asked.

"Under the register," I said. "Floor edge, back slot."

He nodded once. "She stood here with her bag open when she asked about tuition," he said. "Could have fallen then. Or earlier if she held the pad in line to buy tea."

Miss Dotty read the line again, lips moving, eyes steady. "It completes the tale Daria wanted to turn into bait," she said. "Old affair, old heat, no one else's business."

I held the torn edge to the light. The fibers feathered in a pattern we had photographed on another scrap the hospital clerk had bagged for Marin's things. Same pad stock. Same glue ridge. The curve of the tear would meet the first piece if we ever laid them together. We would not do that without her consent. We would still log this one now.

"Chain," I said.

Time. Place. Who saw it. Where it lay. Who lifted it. Photo with masthead. UV check negative. I wrote it on the card and signed across the seam of the small sleeve. Miss Dotty signed under me. Rafi taped it clean and printed a label with the case number and a note in plain words. Marin slip, closure line, found under register.

Peppermint sniffed the empty slot, decided the work pleased

him, and flopped against the receipt roll with the sigh of a clerk who met quota.

I read the slip one more time and let the last sentence land where it should. Not this time. Daria had tried to set a room on a private confession and call it culture. Marin had planned to speak on her own rules and then got shoved and lured and taped for her trouble. The note told the thing we already knew. The first story belongs to the person who lived it, not the person who sells tickets.

I boxed the sleeve with the rest of the file. Pins. Donor sheets. Len's sample. UV strip. Alley stills. Title Office forms. Walter's admission in his own untidy hand. The scuff photo from the trunk. I laid the small crown pin pouch on top because it had started the day's last turn. Then I closed the lid and signed the box tape with a line the city clerk will be able to read when his eyes are tired.

Rafi killed the case light. Miss Dotty pulled the shade on the door. The shop breathed the way rooms breathe when work stands up on its own legs.

I wrote one card for the board. No flourish. No speech. Four lines in ink that will not smudge if a thumb tries.

Firsts matter.
So does first truth.
We keep both clean.
Signed, and dated.

I pinned it where anyone at the counter could see it and went to lock the back. Peppermint chose the windowsill that faces the street and curled into a comma, grammar in fur. Out on the sidewalk a couple argued kindly about dinner. A bus sighed. Somewhere, a phone rang for someone else.

Tomorrow the museum will sit at our table and turn a page with care. Marin will walk past the ramp that tried to take something from her and not taste copper. Walter will stand in his open door and count his days without a plate. Daria will think about rooms that no longer clap on command. Talia will file a bursary form and not owe a sponsor a piece of her spine.

We will open on time. We will answer to dots and dates. We will pour tea and argue about jackets. We will leave the alley camera on. We will keep the first truth in front of the first book.

I put the keys in the drawer. I touched the card on the board. Peppermint thumped his tail once, verdict delivered. Then we turned the sign, and went home.

END OF BOOK THREE
PEPPERMINT CAT BOOKSHOP MYSTERIES

ABOUT THE AUTHOR

Ivy Grant is a celebrated fiction author best known for her gripping mysteries and heart-racing adventure novels that blend sharp intellect with atmospheric storytelling. Born in a quiet coastal town where fog rolled in like secrets, Ivy grew up with a fascination for hidden things—locked drawers, whispered rumors, and maps that didn't quite match the terrain.

Ivy remains famously private, rarely giving interviews and preferring to let her characters do the talking. When she's not writing, she's said to be hiking through storm-lashed moors, sketching story ideas on café napkins, or cataloging antique keys she insists will someday open something extraordinary.

THANK YOU.

Printed in Dunstable, United Kingdom